I Don't Like Coffee, I Like You

A BL Coffeeshop Romance

April Klasen

Independently Published
2024

First Printing: 2024

Paperback ISBN 978-1-923217-96-6
E-book ISBN 978-1-923217-97-3

April Klasen
aprilklasenauthor@hotmail.com

Acknowledgements

I must acknowledge my obsession with the ship MoShang (from the Chinese danmei series The Scum Villian's Self-Saving System by MXTX). **This story started as a half-baked idea of a fic inside of a fanfic I was writing.** Only, I liked the idea. And thus it became the BL coffee shop romance that no-one asked for (though many have asked when I would be continuing the fanfic or if I am even alive to do so).

As always, thank you **mother** for editing and proof reading. At least the smut is toned down in this one.

Dedicated to coffee devotees, tea lovers, and hot
chocolate obsessed gremlins.
Let it be hot and tasty!
(just like that ass)

1. Hot Barista

"What can I get for you?" Hot Barista asked.

Your dick, I thought. *Let me suck it, sit on it, or jerk it off. Whatever you prefer, I am happy to serve you.* "The usual," my mouth said instead. *Yeah, real smooth, Roo. Real smooth.*

"Always the usual for you," he scoffed as he rang up my order of a regular sized coffee to go.

"Don't be mean. I'm a paying customer," I whined and tapped my card to pay the bill before handing over the travel mug.

"So?"

Ohhhhh, down boy. Don't get turned on by the hot barista bullying you.

"So, you could be nice to me," I tried my best to sound flirty. Giving him the best puppy dog eyes I could and pouting with my bottom lip popped out.

Hot Barista snorted and as he took the travel mug, made sure his long fingers grazed mine, even though there was no reason for him to touch me at all. I had offered it over with the handle pointed to him for ease. He'd skipped it. Wrapped around the shaft of the mug and had touched me.

On purpose!

"Why would I be nice to you?" he went over to the coffee machine and started the order.

"Because I'm your best customer," I raised my voice to be heard over the roar of that machine.

"Sounds like a you problem," he retorted. "I've never been nice, yet you still come."

Excuse me?! Ohhhhh calm down. Easy, Roo. Easy. Don't get ahead of yourself.

"Ahh…" I felt my face get rather flushed over that comment and I may have lost the ability to respond to him. So, I let him win, this round of our little verbal sparring. And watched him as he worked on my order.

Fuck me, he was hot. Hence the name Hot Barista.

Taller than me. Muscular, which was insane. Why did he need to have biceps that looked chewable? The sleeve of his black work shirt stretched around it taut and *fuuuuuuuck.* And then his waist. It was the shoulder to waist ratio that made him look like he was a corn chip. Like I wanted to wrap my legs around his middle and cling to his shoulders.

Inky black hair that was pulled into a bun at the top of his head with wispy bits falling free and framing his face. Dark brown eyes. Features that said his heritage was somewhere from Asia.

Altogether, he was attractive. Add on his personality and I was doomed to be a spluttering idiot with a crush and no hope, yet I still try to flirt.

So yes, my own problem.

But I still come back every day when I could to get a coffee to go and spend some time with Hot Barista.

"You could try something new, I can make you a different drink," he huffed as he finished up the order and screwed the lid back to the travel mug with those long, slender fingers.

"Aw, are you wanting to show off to me?" I teased back.

"I'm just bored with always making you the same thing," he drawled, returning to the counter and sliding the drink over. Hands free, he placed them to the surface and leaned. Staring me down.

I took the cup. Flicked the little bit that covered the mouth and brought it close to my nose, inhaled and sighed in appreciation. Added a little moan to it. Just to tease.

"And?" he quirked his brow at me.

"Smells good," I told him, trying for nonchalance. The steam wafting through that little gap carried that heavy scent of coffee that was roasted perfectly, I think. I grinned at him. "Thank you."

"You're welcome," he replied. "Don't burn your tongue. Let it cool before drinking."

I rolled my eyes at him. "One time."

"Yeah. You're a full-grown adult that needs to be given warnings about hot beverages. Blow on it." Hot Barista said without shame and a straight face. Just deadpanned.

Thank fuck I wasn't drinking it or else I would be spluttering.

Again, my face felt hot as Hades and I lacked words to come back to that. *What the Hell?! Ahhhhhh!*

Behind me, the bell of the door rang and new customers entered. I raised the cup into the air and started to turn from the counter. "See you tomorrow."

"I'll be here."

I retreated from the small café. Without his number. Again.

"I'm such a loser," I complained under my breath to myself. But would I be ruining everything if I did ask for his number? If I popped into the café one morning on the way through to work and asked him 'are you queer and single?'

Just because I thought he was flirting back with me, didn't mean he was.

He could be just passing the time with banter with someone he's found who isn't easily offended. Or this is his customer service personality. Or he could be queer but had a partner.

Or he might be looking for just a one-time thing.

Which wouldn't be so bad except I didn't want it to be once…

Or I am over thinking it all like an idiot and should get over myself. He's just a guy. A hot guy, sure. But still just a guy. And if he'd wanted to, he could be easily asking for my number. It's not like I don't flirt with him!

I entered my office building. Juggling with my coffee to get my security badge out of my pocket to scan it and enter.

"Morning," I called to the receptionist, Ronda.

She smiled at me. "Good morning, Roo."

"Any hot gossip?" I flashed her a dimpled grin and leaned in close when she grinned back.

"You didn't hear it from me," she warned.

"You? Never seen you before in my life. No idea who you are."

She looked around before divulging all of what she'd over heard and witnessed while working the reception desk. Her words spilled like wonderful hot tea.

I gasped. "No!"

"Yes!" she insisted. "And he had to be escorted off the premises and into police custody. Happened right in front of my desk."

"I never expected that of him," I hissed back, my eyes darting around to make sure that we were not the object of eavesdroppers. "What are they going to do?"

"His computer has been seized and they're going through searching every room."

"Are you alright?" I asked.

She nodded. "I'm fine. They found no cameras in the loos down here. It's just unnerving. I would never have pegged him as being a sicko."

"Neither did I. But I guess we can't judge based on appearances. What's the talk about how they're handling it?"

"Keeping it quiet for the moment. There's a police investigation. So they can't just make a big announcement."

"They're gonna have to say something," I insisted. "This isn't someone stealing toilet paper. This is a serious crime and the employees need to be made aware of it. Transparency and everything."

Ronda nodded. "Worst thing is, all of the victims are going to have to watch these videos to confirm that they are the ones in them."

I hissed through my teeth. *Shit.* "This is bad. On so many levels."

"We could be on a sinking ship," she warned.

"Hmm," I tapped my fingers against the travel mug in my hands. "What's your gut telling you about this?"

"Start looking for a back-up," she answered immediately.

"A back-up to what?"

Ronda and I turned to the new comer and hissed at them to keep it down.

Ash winced.

Again, Ronda spilt the tea. And this time, I had to slap a hand over Ash's mouth to keep them from yelling. I nearly spilt my coffee in the process.

"Shut up," I hissed.

Ash grabbed my wrist ripping my hand free from their mouth and glared. "Are you kidding me?! That was what that creep was doing?! And they're not going to make a fuss because of an ongoing investigation?!" Luckily, they'd kept their tone lowered.

Ronda shrugged. "This is all I've heard. And seen. I don't know. Maybe if you go to your desk, you'll find an email or something."

Ash grumbled. Grabbed my elbow and started to haul me along.

I waved back at Ronda. "Bye."

Ash stabbed the button for the elevator and practically vibrated in their rage as we waited. "This is bullshit!"

"I know," I sighed. Trying to comfort them.

"I just can't believe this shit is what I'm coming into today. Ugh. Fucking hell. I'm quitting," they announced to me.

"Maybe wait and see what happens," I cautioned

"Fuck that," they snapped.

The elevator dinged and the doors opened. We jumped on, followed by others who worked upstairs and thus we had to keep our mouths shut.

Once on our floor, and as we walked towards our little cubicles, we continued to talk. Hushed. Barely audible.

"We can do it," they insisted. "Leave and start our own business."

I sighed. "In this economy? I like to be able to pay my bills, thanks."

"Don't be a wuss," Ash complained. "We'll be unstoppable. And we'll take Ronda with us."

Not a new idea. We'd been kicking around the concept of starting our own business for years now. Always around the time something was fucking up at work. Always imagining having our own thing. Something we could control and make our own hours for.

Candles.

Stickers.

Hell, we'd even discussed the merits of selling sex toys.

But ultimately, we lacked something very important. Money, yes. But passion. We had nothing we were passionate about and it showed in the way we'd easily jumped from one idea to the next. One new product to the next, following a trend.

"Skippy!"

I didn't respond.

"Skip!"

Again, I didn't respond to the name.

Beside me, Ash looked ready to yell back. But I gripped their forearm in warning.

"Skip," this time it was right behind me and accompanied with a tap to my shoulder.

I sighed. "My name is Roo."

"Like a kangaroo," the idiot Johno explained. "That's why I call you Skippy. Skippy the bush kangaroo."

"I don't skip," I gritted my teeth. How many times had we had this fucking conversation? How many times had I told him to use my damn name? Roo was already a nickname.

"Obviously," Johno chuckled.

Bitch! Leave my beautiful chubby body out of this. Now I turned to glare at him. "What the fuck do you want?"

"Whoa there. No need to get hostile."

"No need for you to be so stupid. Yet here you are," I retorted. Whatever good mood I'd had before entering this building had been chipped away by the news from Ronda and now was bulldozed completely by this idiot I had to work with.

With. Not for. He was not my supervisor.

"Boss wants to see you in the office, I'm just passing on the message," he said and walked away.

"Asshole," Ash hissed at him. Quietly.

I nodded with them. Dumping my things off on my desk, I headed straight to the office of my manager. My boss.

Emily looked up from her computer and motioned me in. "Close the door, please Roo. And take a seat."

"Should I be worried?" I asked, perching on the chair.

"What have you heard?" she looked at me from over her glasses perched on her nose.

I grimaced. "That someone was hiding cameras in the ladies' bathrooms."

"And their employee contract here has been terminated," she confirmed.

"Should you be telling me this?" *Why was she telling me this? What the hell is going on?*

"Management is about to call a workplace wide meeting and announce what has been discovered and what it means right this moment. It's going to be a shit show. But that doesn't mean we don't have projects that can be put on hold."

"Okay," *corporate hell.* Sure, someone's rights were violated in the workplace, but the job still has to get done.

"I want to recommend you for the manager position."

She dropped the bomb.

It exploded in front of me.

And I gaped at her. "Huh?" Not my finest moment of mental clarity.

"Roo," she warned.

I shook my head. "Sorry. But what on earth?!"

She leaned back into her chair and started to massage her temples. "I need someone I can trust in that position."

I was chuffed at that little praise. It was nice. Emily had been my supervisor from the start. She'd trained me and covered my ass when I fucked up early on. Which I tried not to do. But she was a great supervisor. And a great manager. I liked working under her.

Then I frowned.

"Trust? What do you mean need someone you trust?"

She paused. "There is another option that could be recommended. But they're not someone I would ever want in a managerial position. Let alone one that has opened up because of a scandal like this."

I racked my brain trying to think of who she was hinting at.

"I need you to say yes," she pushed.

I huffed a sigh and sagged into my chair the same way she was. "Is it going to be just temporary?"

"I don't know. That would depend upon you and how well you survive under the circumstances."

"And if I refuse…"

"Then someone else is getting the position and that's going to explode in our faces," she admitted. "Please Roo."

"What's HR offering for the position?" I asked. Might as well make an informed decision.

She handed me a print out and began to talk about the increase in pay and what not. "A copy has been emailed to you. But I need an answer sooner rather than later."

I swallowed.

Hesitating over something like this? What was I doing? Except, I didn't want the added stress of managing a whole ass project. And jumping in part way through? *Shit.*

I opened my mouth. "I want to take Ash with me onto this project."

Emily frowned. "Manager position is the only one allowed to make that request. Does that mean you're saying yes?"

I still hesitated.

I always hesitate.

But I chewed my bottom lip.

Emily nodded. "Think about it. Get back to me. Preferably before the end of the day." And with that she dismissed me and I left her office.

Ash poked their head over the cubicle divider and looked at me as I sat in my office chair, making it groan under me harder than I was groaning.

"You good?" they enquired.

I motioned them over to my side and in a hushed tone explained.

Ash widened their eyes. "You want me to go with you?"

I nodded. "I'll do it if you want to jump into it."

Without hesitation, Ash nodded. "Let's do it! Call Emily now. Or we can go to her office and tell her."

"Calm down," I held onto their elbow to stop them from grabbing my chair and dragging me along behind them to Emily's office and officially accept it. "What happened to you wanting to quit?"

"We can quit when the next lot of shit hits the fan," they conceded. "Or if we come up with a proper business plan. Until then, let's get the extra pay."

Management sent out a mass email about a meeting in five minutes. The whole office started to buzz with the possibility of what they were announcing. Scary words like 'letting go' and 'bankruptcy' floated around.

Ash and I shared a look.

"May I have everyone's attention," Our boss-boss called out over everyone. "As some of you have heard, we've had an unfortunate incident occur and one of our managers has been… implicated. An official police investigation is underway and I cannot talk too much about it. It is horrible what happened. We are like a family in this company."

Do not roll eyes. Do not roll eyes. Do not roll eyes.

"And it hurts me greatly to say that one of our own was allegedly doing such a thing to us. But that doesn't mean that we can give up. We have people here for you to talk to about how you're feeling on all of this. Be reassured we've done everything to ensure your safety and have checked diligently for any other hidden cameras."

"Cameras?" Someone cried out on the other side of the room.

Clearly, they were unaware.

Boss-boss cleared his throat. "Ah, yes. I guess I have to admit. Cameras were found hidden in places. The recordings were stored on a manager's desktop. And we're handling this all to the advice of the police and legal department."

I winced at that. Not very sincere. Nor awe inspiring.

The general populace was once again buzzing away, now that it had been confirmed as to what was going on. What had happened.

Emily looked over to me and raised her brows in question.

What? She wanted an answer like this? No way. Nope.

I was already reevaluating my half choice I'd made. Did I really want to get myself involved here with this mess? It was bad enough I worked in this company to begin with. But to become one of the managers, one of the many who kept the same old company running as usual and not changing anything for the better?

Oh fuck.

Ash was right. We should quit and start our own thing. Take Ronda with us. Sell candles or dildos or anything! As long as it wasn't just helping them to exploit under the guise of being a 'family business.'

I hesitated.

To nod or shake the head. For that is the question.

"Luckily," Boss-boss continued talking. "We've already secured a new manager and they'll step into the position effective immediately."

I frowned.

Emily frowned.

Johno stood up and came forward as the boss-boss motioned for him to. Clapped him on the back. Announced it loud and clear that the new projects manager was to be Johno and how proud he was to have such a great man taking over in such dire times.

Emily gaped.

Ash poked me and gaped.

I gaped back.

"That's all," boss-boss dismissed.

We watched Emily pounce and talk with them quickly and quietly. Her outrage became more and more evident with her shoulders near her ears, jaw clenched, and hands flying about the place.

They'd undermined her.

"There goes our pay rise," Ash sighed.

"Typical," I grumbled. "We never get anything good."

"The plight of minority communities," they added on. "Would this classify as a hate crime?"

"What?"

"You know, since you were offered the job but it was given to someone else before you could accept it."

I huffed a laugh. "If you can find proof it had been done because of my sexual orientation. Then yes, it would be an act of discrimination. But that would be near impossible to do. It's not like they'd be recording themselves cackling away and making their evil plot to keep the gay man chained to his desk as a lowly clerical worker as they give the promotion to someone else."

Ash pouted.

"Go get to work," I told them. "We're still getting paid to do said lowly clerical work." As I said this I reached for the travel mug and popped the lid over the mouth piece and sipped the coffee.

Grimaced.

I don't like coffee. Fuck. I really don't like coffee. But I do like Hot Barista. And so I sipped more.

2. Don't Cry Over Spilt Milk

"You're late," Hot Barista snapped as I entered.

I smirked at him. "Were you afraid I wasn't going to be coming at all?" I teased.

"Wouldn't be my problem if you didn't come."

What is with the word play, hmm? I'm not going insane right and he's using words that could have that other meaning, right? Please God, don't be fucking with me.

"Are you sure that's something you could be proud of?" I bit my lip before adding. "If you couldn't make me come?"

Of course, the store was empty!

No other customers except for myself. The tables were all open and no line up to the counter nor people milling about for their order. Empty. Alone. Just us two. I could hear someone out back in the kitchen, but they didn't matter. They weren't in the room.

Hot Barista's lip curled and he looked me up and down. Slow.

Holy shit. I stood straighter. Tried not to fidget. "Like what you see?" Bold. Maybe a little bratty.

"Hmm."

"Hmm?"

"You look at me and never compliment."

What? "Would you like me to?" This time, a nervous little laugh started to bubble out. And I fidgeted. Picked at my nails. Chewed my bottom lip.

Hot Barista's eyes zeroed in on that action. "What would you say?" he prompted.

I swallowed. Hard. *Fuck me.* Okay, this was teetering close to the edge of being inappropriate. Completely inappropriate for the workplace and for what you could classify as harmless flirting between a customer and barista.

This wasn't normal.

Again, a nervous laugh and my hand came up to rub at the back of my neck. "Probably nothing I could say out loud. Good thing you can't read minds. Or else you'd be kicking me out and banning me from this place." *Whoa! Don't admit too much like that!*

"Say it out loud," he pushed.

I blinked at him.

This was like consent, right? He wanted me to… to tell him how thirsty I was for him. "Are you sure?" I asked.

He softened a bit with that. Just on the edges. "Yes. I want to know what you think when you're checking me out."

My face burned. My eyes dropped down to check him out. The filter on my mouth held firm and luckily I wasn't blurting out how attractive I found him, how I wanted him, all of the different ways he could have my every orifices, maybe I wanted to marry him, definitely wanted to try motor boating his fat pecs.

"Um…" *So eloquent.*

He cocked his brow and pushed. "Use your words."

Ohhhhhhh… "Will you call me a good boy if I do?"

…

…

Oh fuck.

I said that part out loud! *Shit!* My face was now on fire and I buried it into my palms. Crying in despair.

But his smooth chuckle filled the air between us. "You have to do something good to get praise."

Oh?!

My hands lowered. I peered at him.

"I don't praise brats."

"What do you do to brats?"

"Exactly what they want me to do," and he placed his palms onto the counter and leant forward. "What they've asked for."

"Are you a…" I trailed off.

He snorted. Pulled back and crossed his arms over his chest. "You're dodging the original question."

"Which is not half as important as knowing if you are a member of the kinky community," this time, I sounded normal.

And it must've told him that this was a conversation time and not a flirty one, because of the huge sigh he gave and then the way he motioned me closer to the counter. "Sorry about that."

"What?"

"Well, I did start to say shit without knowing if you were into it."

"I was into it," I announced very quick and clear. "I was very into it. But… like, are you a dominant? I've never seen one in the wild. At least not a real one."

"Switch."

Ohhhhhh.

"You know about dom/sub dynamics?"

"More than thermodynamics," I teased. But still nodded. "Something about it. I'm um… very vanilla."

"Vanilla is valid."

"Says the guy who sounds like he would put me over his knee and paddle my ass."

Hot Barista chuckled again at that. "Not unless you asked for it before."

"So consent."

"And boundaries."

"Cool."

We lapse into silence. Where do we go from here? What do we do? How do we act when we know this now? When the conversation has turned in such a direction? Go back to flirting and acting like nothing has changed?

Or…

"What can I get for you?"

"The usual," I say and go through the normal routine of paying and handing over the travel mug. "It's quiet today," I commented.

He doesn't look up from his task of preparing my order. "You're late. And customers will start to come in soon."

"Yeah, I was in a rush this morning and couldn't stop. But my manager sent me out on an errand and I wanted to see you… make my coffee. I wanted coffee," I stuttered.

Dark eyes glinted as he looked at me. "Right."

"Shut up," I mumbled.

He chuckled, but the screaming of the coffee machine buried it and I was disappointed not to hear it. His lips moved again. I could just make out the sound. He looked over and noted my confused face and repeated, louder. "You work in an office?"

Small talk. Didn't see that coming. "Um, yeah. Just a boring office worker," My hand waved over the button-down shirt tucked into nice slacks and corporate appropriate shoes.

"Don't like it?"

"What do you mean?"

"You sound like you don't like it."

I shrugged. "It's a job."

"Just eight hours of your day, every work day."

"Didn't think we were going to be talking philosophical. Normally it's flirty."

"Do you want to just flirt?"

"No… not just flirt," I tried to imply in my tone that I also wanted to talk about other things. That I wanted to get to know him and not just wanting to be intimately acquainted with his dick. "Do you like working here?"

He nodded. "Yes."

"Have you always wanted to be a barista?"

"No. But that doesn't mean I don't enjoy it. Or that I don't find it a fulfilling career option for the moment."

I frowned at that. "You're not going to stay?"

"Why would I stay in one job forever?"

"Job security?"

"Boring."

"It's boring to know that you're going to be able to pay your bills and eat each week?" What on earth is with this guy? Maybe we should've just kept it at flirting.

"You live pay check to pay check?"

"No…" I grimaced. "I try not to."

My coffee mug filled and lid secured, he returned to the counter. But didn't immediately hand it over. He watched me.

I huffed. "Are we really discussing finances here and now? What happened to the flirt?"

"Are you afraid to talk money?"

"It's rude to ask about someone's finances," I retorted. "Never ask how much someone makes. It's like asking someone's weight."

His eyes flicked down again, looking at my body. "If I ask for your weight it'd be so I could tailor my workout to make sure I can bench press it. And more."

"Whoa…" My eyes went wide. But my imagination started to think of all the kind of things this man could do if he could lift me up. Easily. Hold me up in the air.

"But…" Then he straightened.

The bell on the door jingled behind me and a cacophony of noise followed. Turning I found a group of mothers with prams and children off the lead and running about them. I hurried over to hold the door open for them.

"Thanks!" one mother said to me before turning to a child. "Brady, honey. Don't touch that."

I should escape now. I should slip out this door and leave, maybe give Hot Barista a wave, but definitely leave him to his work.

But my travel mug was still on the counter. And the mothers were mobbed in front of it.

"Abby, counter," Hot Barista yelled.

"On it," a voice came from back and a short woman strutted out, took one look at the crowd and leapt in.

They worked well together to get through the orders. Directed the mothers to sit wherever they wanted and they'd bring the orders over.

I loitered nearby. Wanting my travel mug. Unable to push my way forward to grab it.

Hot Barista noticed. He grabbed the mug and motioned me to come to the side of the counter, almost around to his side of it. I stepped.

But hadn't looked down.

A small child with a hot beverage in their hands *(who was the idiot to give a child a hot drink?!)* collided with me or I with them and the contents dumped over my slacks.

"Shit!" I hissed.

"What did you just say to my son?" A woman bellowed.

I started to tug at the fabric to rip it from close contact with my skin. *Fuck that was hot! Not the fun hot. Not the fun hot!* I glared at the brat and now the woman trying to get into my face about it. "He spilt something hot onto me. It's a reaction to swear."

"He's a child."

"Still, hot beverage on me," I fired back.

Said child started to bawl their eyes out.

Great. Thank fuck homosexuality was it's own form of contraceptive and I never had to worry about having an oopsie baby.

Hot Barista swooped in and took my arm. "Come with me." He paid no heed to the mother still bitching about me being rude to her precious little brat. Just tugged me along behind him to the back of the café. He pushed me into a bathroom. "Strip," he ordered and then closed the door.

I undid my belt and pants and pushed them down.

Better. Fucking hell. It was better. But as I looked at my thigh, it was red and splotchy and stung. What was I meant to do with a burn? Hold it under running water?

I looked at the small hand sink. How the hell was I going to get my leg up and into there?! And wasn't there like a time thing? I had to hold it under water for so long? I can't remember.

And my slacks! Ah, they would be stained after this and ruined.

I bundled up paper towel and started to soak it under a stream of icy water before squeezing out a bit and applying to my skin. It stung.

I hissed.

The door opened again.

Panicked, I look over.

Hot Barista.

Oh fuck. "Don't scare me," I complained. "I thought some mother was bringing their kid in here and I was going to be yelled at for indecent exposure."

"Hmm," he locked the door. It was almost like a snarky comment on it's own, the click of that lock into place.

I looked at the first aid kit in his hands. "Do you have any burn cream?" I asked.

"Yes. Move your hands and let me see."

Excuse me? My hands did not move from where they were holding the wet paper towel wad to my thigh. "Um," I cleared my throat. "I think I can do it myself. Thanks."

My free hand reached out to take the first aid kit.

But he ignored me and came over. Dropped to his motherfucking knees in front of me and *oh God!* He grabbed my wrist and forced my hand out of the way. "Stop being a brat and let me help."

"A brat? I'm not being a brat. I'm trying to take care of myself. What are you doing?" My voice squeaked. How could it not when a gorgeous man was on his knees and my pants were bunched at my ankles. *Lord above and Satan below. Think unsexy thoughts. Don't give me a surprise boner right now! Please!*

"I have first aid training," he deadpanned at me.

"And did your training tell you to get on your knees when a guy has their pants off? Get up!" I reached over to grab his shoulders and try to haul him up. Froze. *Whoa. Whoooooooaaaaa.* Solid muscle. Body heat radiating off. And something about… well, um… about touching him in a way that's not a casual brush of fingers in public. And even worse when it's in this position.

Hot Barista glared at me. Pinched my uninjured thigh.

I yelped.

"Head out of the gutter for five minutes," he chided. "How bad does it hurt?"

"It's painful but not like I'm crying or anything."

His fingers touched the skin around the burn as he inspected. "It isn't blistering."

"Oh good. You're a doctor," I tried to roll my eyes, make out like this was a joke. But he was touching my leg!

"First aid training. And we get a lot of burns from the coffee machine," he explained. Opened the kit and pulled out burn cream. "Are you allergic to anything? On any medication?"

"No."

Popped off the lid and squirted a generous amount to his fingers and…

"Ahhh!" I yelped.

"Stand still," he ordered and smeared it all over the area. "I'll put a wet bandage over it for now. Do you want to go to the hospital?"

I squirmed as he worked away. "Nah. It's not so bad. And it could be hours waiting to be seen by a doctor."

"Honestly, they'll just do the same thing and use the burn cream. But you might still want to get it checked out."

"I'll think about it," I chewed my bottom lip. "Are you finished?"

"Did you get hit anywhere else?" Without waiting for a response he started to push my shirt tails out of the way and looked higher.

"No!" I guarded my junk with my hands. "My dick is fine."

He froze.

I froze.

"I meant any splashes onto your other leg or your stomach."

…

I groaned in embarrassment.

He snickered. Added the wet bandage over my injury. Stood up. Turned to the sink and began to wash his hands. "Do you want some ibuprofen for the pain?"

"No thanks. I'll be alright." It hurt to bend and pull up my pants. I tucked in my shirt and did up the zipper. Buckled the belt. Chewed my lip some more.

What a way to spend the morning. *Shit.*

Hot Barista dried his hands on paper towel. "Are you okay?"

"Yeah."

Silence.

It stretched out. Long. Shouldn't he be leaving to go back to work? Didn't he say that they were expecting customers to come in this time of day?

I side stepped him and moved to the sink. He only stepped back enough to let me in front of him. Lord, the way he crowded over me… *whoa.* The way it felt to have him that close.

Did I dare look at him in the mirror?

Temptation won. I looked.

He was staring back at me.

I blinked. "What?"

"Take it off."

"Take what off?"

"Your pants," he ordered.

"Why would I…" but then he pressed against me. His body to my back. *Oh. Oh!* "Oh."

"Take it off," he repeated. "Unless you want to leave," as he said this, he swayed away from me.

And I panicked. "No," I swayed to follow him and keep him pressed against me. Dropped my head back onto his shoulder and tilted to brush my forehead to his throat. "I don't want to leave."

His voice rumbled through his chest and into me as he spoke next. And that shiver that raced up my spine because of it…

"Good." He reached around and rested his hands on the buckle of my belt. "But if you don't do it, I'll do it for you," he warned. But he didn't proceed.

He waited.

"What are you waiting for?" I asked him. Confused only slightly, because I got the feeling that he was waiting for my consent. And fuck that was hot. The good kind of hot. The moan out loud and bend over and invite him to take me hot.

"I want you to say it." Though his hands were very in-appropriately placed on my persons, the heat coming off of them could be felt through my stained pants, they would not intrude further without my verbal consent.

"Please," I begged.

"Please what?"

"Please take them off for me and touch me."

Now he chuckled. "Good boy."

Hmmmmm! The fingers on this man worked slow. Pulled and tugged and released the buckle of the belt. A slow drag of the length of leather coming out of the belt loops. Clattering to the floor.

The pop of the top button.

Slow slide of the zipper.

"Don't tease me," I whined. My hips bucking forward to seek out his hands.

"Impatient," he scolded.

"I have to get back to work," I informed him. "So do you. So please, hurry." I moaned as the pants parted and gave me a little relief for my dick as it hardened in this erotic game of chicken.

"Oh? Is that for me?"

Again, his hands didn't touch, they waited on my hips. Thumbs rubbing in circles. Waiting.

I panted. "Don't pretend like you don't do it on purpose," I snapped back. As best I could. Lord, I was getting desperate. It itched under my skin. Made me want to arch my back and press my ass into the barista's crotch and tempt him with it.

"What was that?" the barista's grip tightened hard on my hips. Stilled any motion that may have started.

I gasped.

He nipped my earlobe and softened his grip, rubbing little circles once more. "You're right, we don't have time to play."

"Don't stop!" I yelped. My hands going to grab his wrists. "Please, don't stop. We can be quick." Arched my back, just how I wanted to. I knew my ass was amazing and could tempt anyone. And found...*Holy shit!* I found Hot Barista hard too. And big. Holy hell, he felt huge against my ass. *Imagine what it would be like inside...*

"Look at me," Hot Barista ordered.

I did. In the mirror, but he clicked his tongue and one hand came up to take me by the jaw and turn and lift my face to kiss me. Hard. My lips parted and tongue flicked out to meet his. *And fuck me! Yes! Yes! YES!*

His free hand came down and pulled my cock free of my underwear. Stroked with his unfair huge hands. Dry. And uncomfortable.

I squirmed.

He pulled his lips away but I chased after him, only to have him chuckle at me. "Spit," he commented. Licked his palm and he brought it back to my dick.

Made me feel good.

I wanted him to feel good with me.

Blind, I reached behind me for his pants and undid them and reached for the thing inside that I wanted so bloody bad. Oh boy. Come here, my little beast. Made my fist into a tight channel for his hips to buck and fuck into.

Each thrust knocked into me and caused me to thrust into his hand and… *hmm.. fuck…* getting there.

I squeezed tighter. Precum leaking from his head made the slide easier.

I whined high in my throat. "Please, oh fuck, please."

He gasped against my temple. Mouthed at the skin there. "Beg, baby. Fuck. You sound so pretty when you beg."

In a moment we both found our release. Mine shooting from his fist and arching in the air to hit the sink. His… hitting my fucking shirt. God damn it.

The high was nice. The clean-up… we awkwardly wiped down with paper towel. I tried to sponge it off my clothes with a wad of wet paper only smearing and leaving little paper fibres behind, so I gave up. Tucked my shirt in and did my pants up. Maybe no-one will notice.

He was back to normal with ease.

He led the way out of the bathroom and back to the front of the café, which was busy. Very busy. Handed me the travel mug that we'd abandoned and immediately plunged into the fray of customers that seemed to fill the small café.

I didn't stick around. I didn't even wave.

I left and thought of probably never being able to go back again. *Fuck. What had I done?!*

3. Back of the Theatre

Okay, so that hadn't been my smartest move. Mutual jerking in the bathroom of a café with Hot Barista. Definitely not smart. Maybe even possibly dumb.

And worse thing… I wanted more. Fucking Hell, it had been one of the hottest experiences of my pathetic gay life and we didn't even fuck. Just him bossing me around, giving me the five knuckle shuffle while I attempted the same for him, and that's all I needed.

But I want more.

I want him.

Now, if I stopped being a coward and went back to the café… But nooooooo, I'm a little wuss and no longer drink coffee to simply have some time to flirt with the guy.

Add in the general bullshit of the rest of my life, specifically work, and it was a very long week and I bloody deserved a treat.

"No."

"What do you mean no?" I was on Ash's side of the divider and talking to them about a late-night viewing at the movie theatre.

"I mean I can't go," they informed me. "Do we need to talk consent, Roo? And what it means when someone says no?"

"Piss off," I reached over and gave their office chair a shove so they spun in place half a turn.

Ash chuckled away at me.

"Skippy," Johno appeared by my side. "Slacking off?" he tsked.

"My name is Roo," I clarified, yet again. Always again. This idiot did it on purpose and that's the annoying thing.

"Right, right," he dismissed. "Did you get that email? You never sent through the files."

"I forwarded it to Emily."

His brow furrowed. "Why would you do that?"

"Because she is my manager," *and I am not working under you, asshole.* "And I have enough of a work load."

Johno looked me up and down and scoffed. "So much work. How can you possibly be able to stop and have an idle conversation on company time with a colleague? What were you discussing? Work matters?"

"Your mother," Ash answered before I could. They were still seated with their back to us. "And why she should've had access to abortions back in her time."

I snorted. Covered my mouth as best I could and failed to hold in the laughter at that. It made my body heave and jerk with the ripples of laughs. Because Ash didn't see, but I saw Johno's face. Priceless.

Speechless.

Unable to utter a single come back to that totally inappropriate comment.

"Get back to work," he ordered and stormed off.

I winced.

He barged into Emily's office.

"We're about to be called in for a meeting," I told Ash. Watched as they shrugged at me. "So, is there a reason you don't want to go and watch a film with me? Or is it just a don't feel like it?"

"Don't feel like it," they admitted.

"Okay."

Ash stopped staring at their computer screen and turned to me. "I'm low on spoons."

"Oh. Do you want me to help out with something?"

They shook their head. "I just want to go home and lay down."

"Okay," I reached over and patted their shoulder.

Ash smiled. Tired.

So yeah, I went to the movie theatre alone. A late night showing of a classic from my childhood. An action adventure with the perfect balance of everything; romance, humour, hot actors. There was a revival for it, a renewed interest in this old story.

And I was going to take advantage and watch it on the big screen. Do I look like a fool? Act like one, yes. Look like one... debatable.

Never mind.

I went to the movie theatre. The final viewing of the film for the day. Wouldn't get out until midnight.

I bought my ticket, some overpriced popcorn and drink combo (because of course I did!), and headed to the viewing room. Best thing, I crossed path with no one! Maybe I'd get lucky and have the whole theatre to myself and get to laugh as loud as I pleased at the ridiculous jokes without being shushed.

The lights were dimmed. Not too much to impair vision, but enough to make it annoying and a little... I don't know, sleep inducing? Maybe.

I glanced at the ticket and saw the assigned seat.

The rows and rows of empty seats almost made it laughable.

Assigned seating in an empty room? Yeah right. And so late at night? Like I was going to behave and follow the rules. The likelihood that another person coming in was going to be looking for their specific seat number and find me in it and then we'd have to have that awkward conversation of 'you're in my seat, please move' was minimal. So low.

And the back of the theatre was always the best spot. Right in the middle of the row. No-one could sit behind you, in front was clear, the screen was perfectly centred.

I went to stake my claim.

Heard the big door to the theatre open.

Shit. Not alone. Was going to have to share with at least one other person. Unless I was lucky and it was just the staff coming in to check before starting the film.

I plopped my ass down into the chair and looked back the way I'd come to find…

Hot Barista.

Mother fucking Hot Barista!

…

My jaw was hanging open. Eyes bugging out to stare at the man I'd been avoiding and never expected to see him here of all places.

He was expressionless. Climbed the stairs up and up and up.

Oh God, was he coming to sit with me?!

Yep.

He did. He took the seat to my right and said nothing. Not even a greeting or an acknowledgement. He sat down and looked straight at the white screen.

My head was turned to him as I stared at his face so up close I could see the stubble growing on his jawline, even in the shitty lighting. A moment passed. Then another. It was awkward.

He sighed and raised his brow at me as he side-eyed. "Want me to move?"

"No," I squeaked out. *Shit.* "You're fine. Just… didn't expect to see you."

"Likewise."

"Um…" I turned back to look at the screen and wait for the projection to be turned on and the trailers to begin.

"You haven't been into the café for a while."

"Huh?" my head whipped back around to him at the sound of his voice. God, I'd missed it. Missed him. It had been less than a week since our little… bathroom incident, but I still missed our interactions. On a whole.

His eyes were trained forward, on the blank screen.

"I um…" I laughed nervously. "Uh." Was embarrassed. Unsure. Want more but don't know how to say it without outright asking. And sure, that's the most logical and efficient way of doing it, but it was also the most scary and vulnerable way possible.

"How's your leg?"

Oh. Concern. Nice. Okay. "It's better. I got a doctor's appointment and had it checked out. Was bitched at for not holding it under running cold water for half an hour, but they still liked the burn cream and wet dressing you did. So um, thanks for that."

"Hmm," was little more than a grunt.

The lights dimmed even further and the projector turned on. Advertisements from local businesses. Shit, even my employer was up on the big screen and I cringed. Is there no way to escape work? Ugh.

Then the trailers for upcoming new releases.

Hot Barista used the arm rest between us. *Asshole!* Everyone knows that's impolite to steal.

I shoved my hand into the popcorn and threw it into my mouth.

"Not going to share?" he asked.

It startled me. It was so close to my ear. And the intimacy that the darkness brought as they turned the lights off completely and the film started with opening credits. I looked over to him. "Are you going to share the armrest?" came out immediately.

He snickered. "Yes." Didn't shift an inch of his arm out of the way.

To use it I would have to be pressed completely against his arm. "That's not moving your arm."

"And you're not sharing," his hand on the arm rest flipped over and his fingers motioned in a come-hither way. "Be nice to me. I make you coffee."

"Ha," I tilted the container in his direction and he took a handful.

He also shifted his arm.

I wedged mine into the space and *ohhhhh.* This might have been a mistake. Hot. Hot body heat from his arm straight into mine. Add in how he shifted to settle more into the seat and I felt it.

My attention was nowhere near the film as the lore of it all was playing out. Nope. Couldn't care how the curse came into being or why it would be a bad idea if someone thousands of years later decided to wake up the bad guy and fulfill the rest of that curse.

All that mattered was Hot Barista. Touching him. Having him reach over and take more popcorn. Then reach for my drink. Slurp from the straw.

"Hey!" I scolded him. "If you want snacks, go get your own."

"But the film has started."

Ass!

Cheapskate!

And I didn't do anything more except grumble about this injustice. And enjoy being pressed against him. And watch one of my all-time favourite films.

I got caught up in the story so much I didn't even notice when Hot Barista threaded our fingers together. Or when he moved our joined hands to his lap. Or that fucking thumb that stroked my hand. Soft. Rhythmic.

I didn't notice anything until I turned to whisper some random trivia fact about the scene happening on screen. "The safety line broke and the actor really was swinging from the gallows," I told him. My eyes still on the screen.

"Hmm?"

I turned my face fully to look at him, or at least glance. Found him giving me his full attention. My eyes flickered to his lips.

No thoughts.

No excuses.

I pushed forward and pressed my lips to his. Realised he'd been holding my hand and I squeezed it tight. Didn't let go. Reached over with my other hand to cup the side of his face and hold him.

Yep, just hold him.

He kissed me back. It was that sort of kissing you did as a teen. Experimenting and seeing what the fuss was all about locking lips and swapping spit, and then finding out that it was nice. Fun.

Then his tongue was introduced to my mouth.

Fun and fuck me! YES! Oh for the love of God, YES!

I tried to keep quiet. But he nibbled my bottom lip. Sucked on my tongue. Shit, this was turning me on. I whimpered. Gasped for air through my nose.

My hand slid up and into his hair, disturbing the man bun he had it in. Loosening it with my fingers. I liked that he rumbled with a moan as I did. It was encouraging.

Hot Barista pulled back from my lips. Tilted his chin down so our foreheads were pressed and we gasped for air together between us. I pushed forward to chase after his lips. To recapture them again. Mine. They're mine and I want them now!

But he tipped to the side and nosed at my cheek. Dragged kisses over my jaw, under my ear, and then…

"Ahhh," I moaned.

He latched onto my throat and started to suck hickies. Each pull went straight to my dick. Made it ache. Made me more of a desperate whore.

My fingers tightened in his hair.

He moved to show the other side of my neck the same treatment.

A boat burning on screen kind of summed up this experience. It was hot and unexpected and all of my brain cells had abandoned ship.

A tug on his hair, encouraged Hot Barista to come back up and kiss me once again. Fill my mouth up with his or else I would continue to whine. He chuckled. Dark. "Cry baby."

Kiss.

"Shut up," I snapped.

Kiss.

"Oh? What are you going to do about it?"

Kiss.

This one was long and drawn out and made me stupid in the head. What was I going to do about it? I don't know. Should I know?

"Hmm?" he prompted. Again, nosing at my jaw.

"Kiss me," I demanded.

"Make me."

I disengaged our hands that had still been entwined on his lap and used that freed hand to grab his thigh, up high. The one still in his hair yanked him back to my lips.

They collided and our teeth bumped. Awkward.

We pulled back with a wince. "Sorry," I let go of his hair and pressed my fingers to my top lip. Tongue pushing on the back of my teeth to alleviate some of the pain.

"Hmm," was all he said. Looked at his lap.

I followed. My hand was so close to his dick! Even in the dark with only the light from the projection illuminating slightly, I could see that bulge. If I moved my hand higher and slipped it inwards…

Gunfire and a flash on screen jerked my attention back to it. My hand pulled away with the move, so I withdrew it from his lap and back to the safety of my own personal space.

Then spotted the mess I'd made. "Fuck," I cursed.

He followed my line of sight and started to snicker at the upended container of popcorn that must've tumbled from my lap while we'd… yeah.

He slurped loudly the last of my drink and sighed as he settled back into his seat.

"You'd better clean that up," he warned.

"Why?" I tried to claim half of the arm rest back. But he shoved me away.

"Seriously. Pick as much as you can up. The staff will be pissed if they have to clean that up right as they're closing."

"But…" I grimaced. "It's dark and I can't see shit. And the movie is…" I frowned. How the fuck had we gotten to this part already?

Huffing a sigh, he fished out his phone and turned on the torch. "Hurry up."

Grumbling, I moved to knee on the sticky *(don't think about it!)* floor. Tried my best not to let my fingers brush it too much as I picked the little individual kernels of popcorn from the carpet and dropped them back into the container. Cried as it took forever. And the fact I hadn't enjoyed as much as I would've liked.

With only a few hard-to-reach pieces left, Hot Barista turned off the flash light on his phone.

I sat back into the seat. Placed the popcorn to the side on a seat down from me and watched the rest of the film. Got to see them rescue the girl, kill the bad guy, and save the world. One last big kiss and they rode off into the sunset with treasure unknowingly hidden on their camel.

Lucky sods.

The end credits began to roll but the lights stayed off.

We sat.

Watched the names of each person involved and recognised for their participation in the making of the film. Listened to the thematically perfect score rise at the end and finish. And still the lights stayed off.

"Did they forget that we were here?" I asked Hot Barista.

"It is after midnight," he stood and collected the cup and held his hand out for the popcorn container. I followed him down the stairs. He ditched the trash into the rubbish bin. We wandered out of the deserted halls in to the lobby. The girl on the counter looked shocked to see us.

"We're the last from that showing," Hot Barista explained.

"Have a good one," she told us and left her post with a little dust pan and broom in hand.

Hot Barista held the door for me.

I smiled at him, closed mouth, as I passed through and out into the night. Sighed. Heavy. "Ahhh, it was so cool seeing it on the big screen like that," I stretched my arms over head. "Not that I got to see a whole lot of it," I side-eyed Hot Barista.

He cocked his brow at me. "You complaining?"

About having his tongue in my mouth for a good portion of a film? Do we breathe air? Should I be concerned about the fact that I felt my face burning and I probably was a blushing mess? As if I were an awkward teen again.

"Only," I cleared my throat. Looked across the deserted parking lot. "If I don't get the chance do it again."

There. I said it. It's out there in the world and for him to do something about it. Laugh it off as a joke. Follow it up with another kiss, even to the cheek. Or…

"I'd complain about it too," Hot Barista admitted.

Or invite me to come home with you. Come on. Do it… or else I'll have to do it. Invite you to come back to my place where we can make out on my lounge for the rest of the night. Stay there if that's all you want, or take it to the bedroom where I tend to keep my stash of lube and you can have at my ass.

"You drive here?"

I shook my head.

Hot Barista frowned. "You're walking home then? At this hour?"

"Walking is good for the body and the Earth," I looked over the carpark again. "I don't see a car for you."

Hot Barista pointed behind my ear. I spun to follow his finger (nice and long and they do feel good when wrapped around my -) and spotted a motorcycle. "Of course you ride a bike."

"What does that mean?"

"It's the aesthetic you give off."

At that he chuckled.

Here it is. He's going to offer to give me a lift home and then I can invite him in and it'll naturally flow and we'll be back to sucking each other's tongues like lollies. *Come on, be a gentleman for this twink!*

"You've ever ridden before?"

"Not a motorcycle," I threw back in a flirt.

"Hmm."

Come on.

...

I swallowed hard. Fuck it. "Are you going to give me a lift home?"

"What happened to walking?" He cocked his brow at me.

"If you give me a ride, maybe I'll let you spend the night." There. That's what you were meant to be doing, you stupid oversized man! Ask me to come over. But no, you're making me do all of that work. Sheesh.

His brow wrinkled.

Oh no.

My stomach dropped away and I recognised where this was going immediately. *Stupid, Roo! Stupid, stupid!*

"I can give you a lift home, but I can't stay over."

Don't laugh and make it into a joke. Don't laugh, you fucking well know it doesn't cover up your nerves. "I'll pass. On the lift. I'm going to walk. Safe trip home," my feet started to carry me away. I waved over my shoulder and booked it out of there.

He didn't stop me.

Once I was on the other side of the carpark I heard him start up his motorcycle, rev it, and ride it out and onto the main road.

I walked home alone and felt… "Fuuuuuck!" I huffed. That was a mess. And embarrassing and I… I don't know anymore. I just don't know.

"As I've said," I repeated. "Emily is my direct manager and I have to send her these things." *I'm not even on your team, fuckwit, why are you sending me work for a project I'm not part of?!*

Johno's vein in his temple visibly throbbed. "I send work to others under her and they just do as I ask. You're the problem," he forced through gritted teeth.

Ash glared at him. They'd jumped on the phone immediately when Johno had loomed over my desk. Called for reinforcements. AKA Emily. Our boss.

"I'm following work flow practices," I forced out to be polite. *Just fuck off.* I want to say it. Want to curse him out because what right did he have to dump his teams' workload onto others who are not part of the project? Just because he's a manager? Ha!

It's not even like I'm sitting at my desk screwing around online, waiting for Emily to assign something. She did assign something. And it was my priority to have that finished before the end of the day. Because that's the job coming down from my manager. My boss.

"We're working for the same company," he snarled back at me. "It's all the same shit. It doesn't matter if it's Emily or myself or another manager. When we give you something to do, you shut up and do it."

Bend.

Flow.

Take the bullshit and find a way to handle it within the timeframe.

Grey rock.

It's just a job.

"That's not how things work here," I snapped back. "You were in the same orientation meeting as me. We were taught that we answer to our own section managers. Not to someone else. If another manager requires more help, they go to another manager and request it. They don't come to individuals and dump their shit on them."

"Roo is right," Emily said from behind Johno. "That is the common practice here."

He swung around to face her.

I realised just how quiet it was in the open space. How everyone in their little cubicles had stopped to listen in. Not that we were being quiet about it.

"That doesn't work," he told her. "And you know it. I'm on a strict deadline. Been thrown into the deep end after the shit that happened. I shouldn't have to go through you to get more help on the project."

Emily gritted her teeth. "Let's discuss this privately," she suggested. "And stop interrupting the peace."

He scoffed. "Fine."

She led him away and after a minute the sound of whispers returned and then the click clack of keyboards.

I huffed a sigh and slumped in my chair. "What the fuck is his problem?!"

"He's targeting you," Ash told me. "I don't see him going for anyone else. You should report him to HR."

"For what?" I stressed. Plunged my fingers into my hair and pulled it. Fuck. "For assigning work to me? For arguing with me when I refuse to do it? That's not bullying. The only thing he's doing wrong is not cooperating with Emily to delegate work outside of his team."

They huffed and started to pout. "When you say it like that, it looks to be reasonable. But this isn't reasonable."

"Isn't it?" If I tug on my hair any more, I'm going to have bald spots. And I do not have the face structure to pull off a bald look. Nope. I fussed and finger combed my hair into place once more. "HR isn't going to be seeing his tone or anything else like that as threatening. They're going to be asking me why I'm not flexible. Why I am pushing back."

Ash fell silent and withdrew back to their desk.

I huffed a sigh and turned back to work. The work that I had been assigned by my manager.

Was I in the wrong for not bending over for just anyone with a fucking manager title? Was I wrong for not being flexible with the rules that the company thumped into us? What the hell?

"Roo?" Emily prompted at my shoulder.

I sighed, again. Looked up at her.

Defeat was written all over her face. She'd lost whatever she had to him. *Shit.*

"Next time John wants you to do something, please, do it. You don't need to run it pass me first."

I grimaced. "That isn't the process here," I tried. But my voice was tired. I was sick of repeating the words and hearing them.

She could see it in me. "Please Roo."

So I nodded. Conceded. I couldn't say it out loud, only give a visual indication to it and then hang my head.

Johno, it seemed, hadn't left. He snickered like an asshole as he watched us. "Do you need me to send through the work again?" He asked.

Oh I wanted to flip him off and tell him to go fuck himself. Instead, I turned back to my computer. "Nah, it should be in my sent folder." It belonged in the trash. "What priority should I make it?"

"Urgent. Needs to be completed by the end of the day," I could hear how pleased he was. It was the worst. Irritating.

"Hold on," Emily did push back. "Roo has work that I've assigned that needs to be completed by end of day. And it is important," she tacked on the last part with a forceful tone. As if she'd been told over and over how unimportant her work is.

John didn't answer right away. I had to look over my shoulder at him to see his grimace. "Assign it to someone else."

What Ash had said stuck out now. I opened my mouth, about ready to start another argument with this information, only to have Johno turn on his heel and walk off. Calling over his shoulder. "Just get it done."

Emily gritted her teeth and looked at me. "Send Ash the work. Divide it between you and just get it done, please."

Ash nodded. "We'll have it finished in time."

Emily left.

Ash and I worked. Hard. Divided the work and still it was so much bullshit to sort through and categorise and organise and type up.

Lunch came. I was tempted to work through it.

Ash whined. "I need a walk, Roo. Walk me."

"You're not a dog," I snapped at them. My fingers flying over the keyboard. My back fucking hurt! Ached. Shit, I'm hunched over. Not to mention my eyes hadn't strayed far from my screen.

"Enough," they came around and dragged my chair, and thus me, away from the desk. Hit save and logged me out of the computer. "Lunch time. Outside. Now. Please."

I huffed and did as they requested.

We left the building. Waved at Ronda as we did. Walked for a while. Until…

"Not this place," I whined.

"Why not? Don't you always get coffee from here? And you were telling me that you wanted to try the food because it always looks so good, but you never remember in time to order something." They pushed open the door and I had no choice but to follow them in.

It was lunch time rush. Filled to the gills. Every table had people. A line to the counter. Three baristas were working to fill orders.

He was working.

Maybe he hadn't spotted me yet, maybe I could get Ash to reconsider and leave.

"Ash…" I hissed into their ear.

"What? Don't want to see your boyfriend?"

The betrayal.

"You little bitch," I gaped at them.

They simply laughed and pointed at some pastries in the display cabinet. "Let's get Ronda a tart. Ohhh, and I want one of those cakes. What are you thinking?"

"How long have you known?" *Wait, that wasn't clearing it up.* "And he's not my boyfriend." I complained.

"You don't drink coffee," They began to explain. "Haven't been on a date in a long time. Oh and I'm a genius and know everything there is to know about you."

"Werido."

They cackled.

We moved up the line.

Hot Barista looked over and our eyes met.

I swallowed hard. Shit. This is embarrassing. What am I doing here? I've already made up my mind to never come back and to avoid him like the plague. Hadn't he been clear? He was happy to fool around when it suited him. But other than that, nope. He wasn't interested.

And that's fine.

But it was also perfectly fine for me to not want to deal with him ever again.

Hot Barista stepped to the counter to take our order. "Long time no see," he said to me.

I let loose an awkward little laugh. "Been busy."

"Hmm," he scoffed. "What can I get you?"

Ash ordered. "I'm paying," they elbowed me in the ribs. "Tell him what you want."

"Um, a sandwich and one of the sugar pastry things," I pointed at something flat and with pink icing."

"Coffee?" Hot Barista asked.

"Please," I said.

Ash at least had the decency not to rib me about that. Fuck them and knowing me so well.

"No travel mug?"

I shook my head. "Forgot it." It was washed up and put away in my kitchen and probably would never see the light of day again. Because I wasn't meant to be back here. At all. *Ash! I curse you and at least five generations of your lineage!*

Hot Barista finished up processing our order. Ash paid. And we hustled to the side to wait for it.

"He's attractive," Ash teased. "And has his eye on you."

"Ash," I hissed. "Leave it be. Please. I'm suffering enough as is without you making me believe in bullshit."

"What do you mean?" they demanded. "Honey, he was looking you over and I didn't even exist… unless something happened and you haven't told me. What happened?!" they pounced on the truth of the matter too bloody quickly.

"Nothing happened," I stressed. Nothing I can admit out loud in a crowded café with the guy right there working on our order!

Hot Barista came over and handed it over. "I'm in tomorrow," he said to me.

"Okay," I didn't say it back.

And it was too busy for him to harass me or flirt with me or whatever.

I hauled ass out of there. Ash followed. Hounded me with questions. It wasn't until we came to the park nearby and sat on a bench that I finally admitted that something did happen.

"But it's nothing," I told them. "We kinda fooled around in a bathroom. Made out in the back of a movie theatre. And flirted. That's it. When I asked if he wanted to…" I trailed off. Left the rest of that statement up to their imagination. "He said no and rode his motorbike off into the night. He's not interested in me."

Ash chewed. "Sounds like you have a communication problem, Roo."

"Don't speak with your mouth full."

Ash swallowed. Took another bite and spoke. "Be up-front with him, coward."

"Sure." I reached for the take away cups. "Which one of these was mine?"

"I think he marked mine to say it had soy milk," Ash commented.

I checked the sides. Noticed that yes, he had written soy onto one cup… but also a phone number onto the other.

"Ash…" my voice was barely over a whisper. They didn't hear me. I had to repeat their name and shove the cup into their line of vision. "What the fuck?!"

"HA! Told you so!"

I stared at it. Hot Barista had given me his number.

"Roo and the barista sitting in a tree, k-i-s-s-i-n-g," they sang like the annoying little shit they were. I felt so sorry for their siblings and the bullshit they'd had to suffer through from them.

"It wasn't a tree," I muttered.

"No, it was the back of a movie theatre like a couple of hormonal teens. And now you have his digits and can booty call him after work. Maybe he does deliveries," they prattled on and on with ridiculous ideas of me calling him up for 'coffee' and having him deliver his dick instead.

"This isn't a damn porno, you degenerate."

"You wish it was."

I balled up the wrapper for my sandwich and threw it at them. They cackled.

"Send him a message."

"Now?!"

"Yes," Ash insisted. "Put his number into your phone so you don't lose it. And then send him something cute. Like a selfie."

"Why a selfie?" I felt self-conscious about doing that idea. Who sent a photo of their face as their first message?

"Because he can then wank off to it later."

"I hate you!"

"Hurry up. We have to get back to the grind," at that statement, we both sighed.

Ash continued to insist on a fucking photo. Tried to snatch my phone away so they could do it for me. I con-ceded with taking a photo of the coffee cup in my hand and writing a thank you message for it.

"Add on that you'll be in tomorrow for coffee," Ash looked over my shoulder, proofreading my work. "And add some pizzaz with an emoji."

"You are too excited by this."

"Yep."

I chewed my lip. Typed what they'd suggested. Wondered if I was coming on too strong. If he was going to just reply with a fucking thumbs up and nothing more. If maybe I should tone it down and just message him back with a 'hi' and see where he took it after that.

"Hit send," Ash instructed.

I did. Locked the screen. Pocketed the phone. And went back to finish up working for the day.

"You still going to drink that?" they asked as I carried the coffee back with us.

I nodded. "It's not that bad. And it's kinda growing on me."

"How much sugar do you add to it?"

I scoffed at that and took a sip of it straight. And the caffeine hit me or maybe it was the taste. But it hit and I woke up fast. Perfect. Maybe it can help to get me through the remainder of the day without losing it and murdering everyone insight and then throwing myself from the window.

Work flowed. It was annoying, but I got done the extra shit Johno had thrown my way. Sent it back to him, made sure to CC in Emily. He replied back to me.

'Thanks, Skippy.'

"Motherfucker," I sneered under my breath.

We finished work. Logged off and left the building. I walked home. Was happy once I was inside and the door was locked and I could kick off my shoes and take off my damned pants and walk around without a care. Sighed to myself.

Got comfortable.

And only then did I check my phone for anything. I had a message from Hot Barista. That's what I programmed him in as. And it suited him.

I chewed my bottom lip as I opened it. Honestly afraid of what his response was going to be. *I swear if it's a damn thumbs up emoji and nothing else, I am blocking his number.*

I refuse to carry a fucking conversation. Not to mention I'm still off kilter about where to stand with him. Like, what did he want? Am I just a convenient hook up?

'Come in tomorrow. Don't forget your travel mug.'

"What?" I frowned at what he'd sent. Was he really giving me an order like that?

'What will happen if I don't?' I asked.

Minutes passed. I tooled around with the idea of finding a movie to zone out to. He responded.

'Stop avoiding me.'

'I'm not avoiding you,' I responded.

Now he sent the eye roll emoji.

'You're the one who didn't want to…' I didn't send that. I deleted it and started again. 'I've been busy.'

'Avoiding me,' he fired back.

'My life doesn't revolve around you. I have a job and it's been such a fucking shit show right now.'

'What's happening?'

So I told him. I explained the situation from the pervert manager with the cameras in the toilets and the fact he had to be replaced immediately and how the higherups circumnavigated my manager who offered me the position and instead gave it to an ass who doesn't follow procedure and though it's all of these little things that happen and make the day long and arduous, it wasn't anything outright that I could point at and say see! Right there! That's the bad guy and the problem and if he was gone it would all be better.

'Sounds like a shit show,' Hot Barista commented.

I snorted. 'You have no idea.'

'Then come see me tomorrow. I'll spike your coffee.'

'You do Irish coffee?'

'No. That's why I'll spike yours.'

I rolled my eyes at that offer. 'I don't drink.'

'Sober for a particular reason?'

'I'm a bad drunk.' *And I don't like who I become when I do get drunk.*

'Then how about you buy coffee for this manager and poison it?'

'Unfortunately, that would be too easy to trace back to me.'

'You're smart. You can think of a way around it.'

'I mean, if I was to do that I would need to get insulin or something and make him OD on that. That way, when they did blood works it would show up that he had high insulin and it would be written off as him not realising he was diabetic and dying from not managing it.'

A moment passed.

'How do you know this?'

'Housemate was in med school when we were in uni.'

The next day… I took the travel mug into the café.

He smirked as I came in. I flipped him the finger as retribution.

"Good boy," he cooed as I came to the counter.

I gagged. "Totally the wrong context for that."

"When would you like me to use it then?" His brow cocked at his enquiry.

Lord, I'd missed this. It was far too easy to slip back into the flirt. And he was gorgeous to look at. I missed him and his stupid little barbs. "Obviously when I've done something good and not when I've been bullied into coming and being a patron for a business."

"Bullied?"

"You bullied me to come back."

"Because you were avoiding me," his brows drew together and he crossed his arms. *Fuck. Muscles. Muscles! Look at those biceps.* "Though I don't know why."

"I wasn't avoiding," I huffed and thunked the travel mug to the counter. "The usual please."

He didn't move.

I frowned at him. "What?"

"If you tell me why, I'll give you a pastry. For free."

Automatically, my eyes went to the display case and at all of the goodies there. But how the hell did he know that was the right thing to dangle in front of me? I grimaced. They looked so good. I wanted the caramel tart with fresh cream. I hadn't had one of those in years. Oh, or that croissant with chocolate in it.

"One."

I looked back to him.

"Two."

Oh he was counting down.

"Three. No more pastry on offer," Hot Barista shrugged.

"Not fair! I was considering which one I was going to choose," I cried out.

He snorted. "Who said you were going to be allowed to choose?"

I glared at him. "Not fair."

"Tell me," he planted his hands on the counter and leant forward. Into my space. "Tell me," he repeated.

"I thought you didn't want me," I blurted out. Like an idiot. My face burned. *What the hell?!*

He frowned at that. "What gave you that impression?"

"Well," I fidgeted with my nails. Looked away.

He took my chin into his hold and brought me back to focus on him and *ohhhhh,* that was hot. That was so sexy of him. What he did just there, with nothing more than…. *Oh my god!*

"You only play with me when it's convenient."

"Play?"

I groaned. *Wrong word, Roo.* "You know what I mean."

"And you would like more than… playing?"

I chewed my lip.

"Your words. Use them, please."

"I want more. I want…" I swallowed. Looking at him while I admitted this was the worst and most embarrassing thing I had ever done. *Agh!* "I want to go on a date!"

"So would I."

I blinked at him. "Pardon?"

"I would also like to go on a date."

"Oh." Shock. This was shock.

He released my face. Put in my order. I paid. He made the coffee. Bagged up some random pastry, I didn't see what it was. Handed both to me.

"How about a film this weekend?" he suggested.

"Haven't we already done that?" I sneaked a peak at what he'd given me. "Nice," I grinned at the tart in the little paper bag.

"That wasn't a date."

I looked back at him.

"That was a coincidence."

"You didn't want to…" I coughed.

"Want to what?"

"You know, at the end of it. You didn't want to go back to mine," I admitted.

"Is that why you avoided me for a week? Because I didn't want to go back and fuck?"

"No! I mean. It wasn't that. You rejected me and it was… I felt like I'd read it wrong."

"You didn't. And I had work the next day."

Ah. That explains it. I nodded my head.

"And the other time you avoided me?" Hot Barista pushed.

"What other time?"

"After the bathroom."

"Oh… I was embarrassed," I also admitted.

He nodded.

"What?"

"I like when you tell me what's happening. I thought I'd fucked up that time." He admitted to me.

"So we're on the same page now?"

"It seems that way."

I started to back away from the counter. "Call me?"

"Call?"

"I like talking to you."

He gave me a smile. "I'll call you."

And I escaped with the biggest grin on my face like a love-struck fool!

5. Movie Date

"I'll buy the tickets," I insisted. "It's your turn to get the snacks."

"How is it my turn to get the snacks? This is our first date."

KO! On the first move. Bastard. I knew I was a blushing mess when he said that. A date. Our first! It made me feel so many different things all at once from excitement and happiness to embarrassment and a little fear of fucking this up and ending with only a first date.

He cocked his brow at me and held the door as we entered the movie theatre.

He'd picked me up for the date. On his motorbike. Strapped a spare helmet to my head and zipped up a leather jacket on me. My knees had wobbled when he'd parked up and helped me off of his bike and that had made him chuckle at me. Stowed away the things and now here we were, entering the building and arguing.

I sighed. "Fine, I'll get my own snacks and you can get whatever it is you want for yourself." Huffy.

"Who said I wanted snacks?"

We came to the counter. I was annoyed with his attitude then and couldn't speak to the girl selling tickets. So when his payment card flashed and was read, it had happened too fast for me to protest.

"Hey," I shoved at his arm. "What happened to me paying for the ticket?"

He shrugged. Guided us pass the line for the snacks. I looked back, mournful. "Popcorn," I pouted.

"Over priced popcorn," he said.

"And? It's a treat."

"Come on," and Lord above, Satan below, Hot Barista wrapped his arm about my shoulders and made me keep pace with his long legs. Got us to our seats. Settled in. Opened his backpack and…

I laughed. "How old are you?"

"Old enough to know that the snack bar in these places is a scam." He started to pull out a selection. Kept his head down as he did so some of his loosened hair fell over his face. "Unless you want popcorn," he mumbled. "I'll go buy you some popcorn."

He started to get up to go and do just that but my hand shot out to grab his wrist. Was he embarrassed?

"This is perfect," I told him. "What kind of snack did you sneak in?"

He sank back into his seat and I watched as his throat worked to swallow. "Most of it is the old pastries from the shop. Whatever was left over."

"Pastries?" I perked up. Gone was my need to reassure him that this was fine and not a bad move. What replaced it was interest. "What kind of pastries?"

And so he presented them to me. Every sort of pastry. He had them all in individual paper bags that crinkled loudly in the theatre. Tarts, cupcakes, muffins, croissants, chocolate eclairs. My eyes went wide and I wanted to inhale them all. Immediately.

"I want that one," I demanded.

He passed over the baggie. "You're cool with this?" hesitancy clear in his voice.

I looked up at him and grinned. "I haven't snuck snacks into a movie theatre since I was kid, but I'm loving this. Thank you."

Blushing. He was blushing! I made Hot Barista blush!

The next thing he pulled out was drinks in thermos flasks. One each. No need to share.

I snorted. "You really came prepared." Paused. "Did you have snacks the last time with you?"

"Of course."

"And yet you insisted on stealing mine?!" *The cheek!*

He laughed.

"You asshole," I hissed at him.

Still he laughed. Handed the flask over and settled in to watch the opening trailers as the lights began to dim.

I took a bite of the éclair and moaned. Surprised myself. Fuck it was so good.

Hot Barista turned to me.

"What?" I took another bite. And nearly died with the pleasure. Had he kept it in a cooler in his backpack? The cream filling was sweet and refreshingly cool.

"Sounds like you're enjoying yourself," he murmured.

"So what if I am?" Oh, I knew what I sounded like. But that didn't mean I wasn't going to play innocent until he commented on it.

"We're not alone," he warned.

"Oh…" my head swivelled to look at the smattering of other people in the theatre with us. All of them who were focussed on the screen and not us. But could probably hear us, hear me moaning. I swallowed. Yep. Not going to continue that at all.

I went to pop the last bite into my mouth, only for my wrist to be snatched and redirected to Hot Barista's mouth.

"It's good," he commented.

"What is with you stealing my food? Are you planning on taking it out of my mouth next time?" I chastised. But felt… turned on. Oral fixation.

"Are you offering?"

I yanked my wrist from his and smacked his arm. "Shhhh!"

I winced at the subtle reprimand and remembered; we weren't alone in the theatre this time. But also, what the hell? The trailers were still playing. We weren't watching the film yet.

Hot Barista placed into my hands another paper packet. "Eat," he insisted.

"Are you trying to fatten me up more?" I teased and did as instructed. Ohhhh! Caramel tart!

"Why would I do that?" he leant in close to whisper this directly to my ear.

I shivered. The gentle brush of his hot breath against my skin, especially just under my ear… hmm, that was delicious in its own way. I wet my lips before responding. "More cushion for the pushin'?"

The film started.

He chuckled. "Behave." Pulled back and didn't look at me again through the film. Fucking tease!

We shared the armrest equally. Ate the snacks until we were full. Drank the mysterious fluids from the flasks which turned out to be decaf coffee, so not great, but not bad.

It was all so sweet of him. And yeah, maybe some would look at it and call him a cheapskate, but to me? This showed forethought. He thought about me and what kind of snacks I could like. The coffee was an unfortunate given since that's what I always ordered and my own fault. But coffee was growing on me. Kind of.

And yeah. I was liking this.

The film was great. It was easy to get caught up in the story and forget that we were in a movie theatre with other people.

Forget until another lot of disgruntled shushes came my way for laughing too loud.

I cringed.

Hot Barista wrapped his arm around my shoulders and brought me in close. "Ignore them," he told me.

And it helped that he wasn't embarrassed by me. I leaned into him, as best I could with the armrest separating us.

The film ended. We watched the credits as others got up and vacated immediately. There was no easter egg surprise at the end though.

"I don't know why I'm disappointed not to see something else," I complained.

"Hmm," Hot Barista cleaned up the empty packets of food and refilled his bag with the two flasks.

"Maybe we've been trained to expect it," I suggested. "After so many films adding something to the end, it's now an expectation to see something. Be it a spoiler or a promise for a sequel. And when there isn't something it's disappointing."

"Are you disappointed with the film?"

"No," I protested and followed him down the stairs and out of the little theatre and back to the hall leading to the lobby. "It was a great film. I loved it." I then launched into all of the things that had caught my attention in the storyline. The twists and turns of it all and why it was such an interesting film. "It's been a while since I've seen something so good," I complained.

"What do you mean?" He held the door for me.

"I mean… don't you feel like films lately haven't been really concerned about having an engaging story line? Or is it just me?"

Hot Barista took a moment to consider this. "What films have you been watching," he moved to lean up against the side of the building, arms crossing over his chest.

I followed him in loitering. It was nice to chat away and not have this all end so soon. So I told him the big budget blockbusters that I'd seen that had left me a little less than satisfied.

He told me about the films he'd seen and why he'd enjoyed them.

Film talk moved to books. Then to a random tangent on paper that he knew an alarming amount about.

"Did you learn that from a past job?" I asked.

He smiled this little one that said this was maybe a fond memory for him. "No. Art school."

"Art school? You went to art school?" I straightened up and stared at the man in a whole new way.

He tilted his head to the side. "Don't I look the part of a starving artist?"

I scoffed. "Nothing of you looks starved."

"Really?"

My finger came up and poked his chest and found it very solid and oh so appealing. Nice. Holy hell, that is nice. "Not starved." My eyes looked up. "You're an artist?"

He shrugged.

"Why work at a café if you could be selling paintings?"

"I like the café. And do you think that art is so easy to sell? Try getting into a gallery without a contact first introducing you to the owner. Try selling at markets or online. Or doing commissions for people who don't value your work and don't want to pay at all and will talk shit about it," he grimaced.

Okay, touchy subject.

"Art is a full-time gig that takes a toll," he admitted.

I didn't know what to say to that. How do you come up with something that could comfort and validate someone's experience when you know nothing about it? Especially when it's a rare moment of vulnerability.

So I bumped my shoulder into his. Stayed pressed against him.

He did something unexpected and drew me into a hug. "If you're going to comfort then do it properly," he groused.

I huffed a little laugh at that and wrapped my arms about his waist. "Is physical touch a love language thing for you?"

This time, his chuckle vibrated from his chest and into mine. It felt fucking good. So good, I wanted him to do it again and again and let me live within his arms forever more! I nuzzled my nose into his collarbone. The top of my head came up to bump his chin.

Hot Barista inhaled deep and released a heavy sigh into my hair. "I don't want this date to be over," he admitted.

"Neither do I," I agreed. I'd like very much for this to last forever. Though, preferably with us ending up at someone's home so we could cuddle in comfort instead of being out in the dark of a carpark pressed against the wall of the movie theatre building.

There was a loud click. It made me jerk in his arms and lift my head from the nice cradle it had been in.

"They're locking up," he informed me.

Sure enough, the outside lights illuminating the signs were turned off and security doors came down over the glass entryway.

"Oh," I pouted. My arms loosened and his did in response. We pulled apart. "Guess this is the end of the date then," I grimaced.

...

"Unless," I chewed my bottom lip. *Come on, Roo. Be brave! What can he do? Reject you yet again?*

"Hmm?" he frowned.

I swallowed hard. "Do you maybe want to… I mean, you're dropping me off at my place, right?"

"That's the plan."

"Then, do you want to…" oh fucking hell, what is wrong with me and not being able to say it point blank?! Why am I so scared of him saying no? "Spend the night? Or at least, an hour or something… maybe… we can keep talking…" I trailed off and wanted to burry my face back into his chest.

"Okay."

My heart stopped for a second there. "What?"

Hot Barista ran his hand through his hair and seemed to cup the back of his neck as he looked at me and nodded. "I'll spend the night."

"Oh…" and then I was fighting that stupid foolish grin again. Why did this make me so happy? Why was simply having him say yes such a… joyful occasion?

He took my hand and tangled our fingers together. I came closer to him so our arms were pressed against each other.

"You're a nervous wreck," he told me.

I glared at him. "You hide it better," I commented.

"I am never nervous."

"Sure, sure," that little shred of bravery that still circled inside of me had me surging up to my tippy toes and trying to plant a kiss to his nose. Missed and hit his chin instead.

He laughed. "Short ass."

"Shut up and kiss me!"

"Nope," he started to walk away, tugging me along with our joined hands.

"Why not?" I whined.

Beside his motorcycle, he unlocked the hardcase that held his helmet and spare one and started to redress me once more for another ride. "Because," he chided as he did the strap up under my chin. "I want to kiss you in a place where we don't have to stop."

Hello libido! That was both sweet and hot as Hades and I too would also like to kiss in a location where we were not forced to stop because of being caught on camera for public indecency. My pout erased, I began to poke and prod him to hurry up.

He chuckled. "Impatient?"

"Very. I would very much like to go home and suck your face."

"Suck my face? Are you some sort of demon?" He didn't rush as he slipped his jacket on and helmet. Got himself onto the bike and then held it steady as I clambered onto the back of it.

I snuggled up against him. Revelled in how nice it was to wrap my arms around his waist and be very up close and personal with him. "Want me to suck something else?" I practically had to shout it to be sure I was heard through the bulk of my helmet and into his.

His shoulders shook with a laugh and he started the bike.

It rumbled under my ass, vibrating.

He kicked the stand back up, balanced and rolled the bike backwards before having enough room to rev the engine and pull out of the carpark space and onto the main road. Taking the way back to my place.

I chewed my bottom lip. Shit, I'm going to put holes in it with my teeth at this rate. Why was I nervous? It wasn't like I was some little virgin *(ha! Haven't been for years)* or that I don't have the supplies to ensure we are very well prepared for any scenario *(hello bulk buying lube!)*.

But it was something else. And I fucking couldn't figure it out.

Or was this not nerves?

Was this excitement mixed with nerves?

Possible. Probable. Not necessary right now as Hot Barista was parking up in the little carpark provided for my building and turning off the beast between our legs. Once again, he helped me off of the bike and stowed away the paraphernalia before turning to me.

I swallowed. Looked him over with my hungry eyes and God give me strength to have my ass tapped by this man! I offered him my hand.

He didn't hesitate. Took it. Followed me into my building, making sure the main door closed properly before coming up behind me up the stairs.

"Don't follow too close," I whispered to him, not wanting to disturb my neighbours.

"Why?"

Because I don't want to be stopping for my door and have you run face first into my ass. Face sitting is not something to be done haphazardly.

"Afraid I'll be looking at your ass?" He whispered back to my silence.

"It's dark, you wouldn't see much."

"True. I can't see." And then he was touching.

I yelped at the contact.

He shushed me. "I can't see where I'm going," he squeezed. Hard. "I'm just feeling my way."

The temptation to stop there and spin around and make out with him on the stairs was overwhelming. Especially when his hand was so huge it cupped my ass perfectly. Who gave him hands that perfect? Who? I want to thank them for this torture.

We hurried to my door. His hand left my ass, unfortunately. I fumbled the key. Opened, shoved him in, locked the door in a hurry and finally, threw my pathetic self at him. Mouth open and oh so ready to be devoured.

He groaned. Both hands this time grabbing my ass and physically pulling me up and letting me slide back down the front of his body.

"Hmmm," I whined in the back of my throat. Shit.

He repeated again. The friction of that slide! It was like humping only hotter because of how fucking strong he was in the upper body to be lifting me and controlling the situation.

Impatiently, I wrapped my arms about his shoulder and on the next lift, hooked my legs about his waist. Getting the memo, he adjusted and easily held me up. Jolting me a little to get me high up on his waist. And then leaned against the door, his weight bearing down onto me. Hands squeezing and releasing, sliding from ass to thighs and back again.

I tangled my fingers into his hair, pulled out the hair tie holding it into a low ponytail and finally twisted and played with it to my heart's content.

Hot Barista panted. "Bedroom?"

My brain was fuzzy. "That way," I gestured with my chin. Obviously it would be further into the flat. Come on. I didn't wait for him to even look around and get his bearings, I went back to chasing and capturing his mouth in another hungry kiss.

Lord, I loved his mouth. The way he huffed through his nose when I was doing something just on the edge and then *hmm* when I did something right.

His mouth was amazing. What else could I be doing with it? Oh fuck me… that list is… hmm.

My hips buck into him.

"You're going down," he said against my mouth.

Yes, sir! I will go down and give you the best… what are you doing?! He lowered my feet back to the floor, but didn't let me drop to my knees. I whined over that. "Noooooo," dropped seductive little kisses to his throat and collarbone. Wet and open mouth. *Come on, Hot Barista, imagine how good it'll feel to have this mouth on your cock. Imagine it with the tongue.*

Strong, demanding hands grabbed my upper arms and commanded my attention.

I looked up to see the man with wild eyes and messy hair panting. "Bedroom. Walk. Now."

Ohhhhhh! Single word sentences. Perfect. I felt smug satisfaction because I did that with just kissing. My mouth had driven him to this point and now we were going to be stumbling to the bedroom. I took his hand and led the way.

Vaguely pointed out the bathroom for reference. Came to the door for my room. Paused. He pressed against my back, hands gripping my hips, nose buried into my hair, and holy hell! He ground his dick into my ass.

I held onto the door frame to steady myself and pushed back, arched my spine and made my ass pop for him to use it as he liked.

He huffed a laugh into my hair, moved to the side and kissed my temple. "Baby," he groused.

I laughed. "Yeah?"

He took a moment. Was humping my ass with a solid concentration.

I hummed.

Then he stopped and walked us into the room, when my feet weren't working, he fucking lifted me off of them and carried me with ease. How?! How is this man able to do that with me? And why was it the hottest thing to have happened to me in my entire life?

With some lonely brain cell that was still functioning, I slapped the light switch as we passed and illuminated the absolute mess I'd left my sheets in from the night before. But at least there were no clothes on the floor. Small wins.

Then he was putting distance between us. Sat me onto the mattress and then sat his own ass down with a good space in between. Why? What had I done to fuck this up already?

My pouting face made him laugh and reach over to cup my cheek. "You look like I'd just murdered someone close to you."

"You're murdering my self-confidence. Come here," I reached for him.

Cheeks flushed. Chest rising fast with each breath. And… yep, a hard on fighting to be freed from his pants.

I licked my lips as I stared at the utter mouth watering treat in his lap.

He chuckled and tilted my head back up to focus on his face. "We have to talk first."

"Nooooo."

"Yes. What do you want, baby?"

Ohhh, pet name. I liked it. "Your dick."

"Top or bottom? Do you want to be top or bottom?"

I didn't pause to consider. "Bottom." Then it clicked. "I prepped before," I reassured him.

His brows went high.

"I was… um, hopeful that the date would end well." Very hopeful and eager for it to end like this.

He nodded, like he was agreeing that this was an excellent way for the date to end and he too was hoping for it to be like this. "Okay, baby. How do you want to do this? How do you want me to fuck you?"

Apparently, there is a god and they send you men like this when you need them. Or maybe a horny fairy god parent.

Filth spilt from my mouth. All of the things I wanted to do. And he nodded and listened. If I was stumbling over my words or sounded unsure, he asked me to clarify or to slow down. But there was a lot.

"Pick or do you want me to?"

Oh, that was an option? The thrill of handing it over to him had my toes curling in my socks and wondering which position he would choose to fuck me in. Everything I'd suggested had been some form of him stuffing me with his dick, so it was all going to be good.

"You pick," I suggested.

He smirked at that. "Do you have a safe word?"

"No…" I trailed off. Remembered that he had said he was into the dom/sub dynamic. That he was a switch. "Am I going to need one?" Should I be worried?

He cupped my face once more. Unconsciously, I leaned into the touch. "It isn't something to be scared of. I'll still stop if you say no at any time. But it's something handy to have. Just in case."

Why is it so… I don't know. Comforting but also hot but also aww? "What should I say then?"

"I like the traffic light system."

"Which is?"

"Green for good. Everything is good so keep going," as he started to say this he reached for the hem of my shirt and tugged it up and over my head. "Orange for slow down and check in. Maybe I'm not doing something right or you're unsure and need me to explain better."

My hands went to his shirt. Pulled at it.

"Red is for stop. And we stop everything and I need you to know it's okay to stop." Hot Barista said. "These are words for you to use, but also for me to use. Do you understand?"

I bobbed my head in a nod.

"Repeat it back to me."

Um, okay. Demanding. "Green is go. Orange is slow down. Red is stop." Simple. Now can I please get some dick?!

"Good boy," he smirked.

I smacked his shoulder. "You're teasing me."

Hot Barista only smiled more.

Naked. I loved seeing him naked. He wasn't cut with muscle, but it was there. Oh boy it was there under a soft layer of flesh. The muscles were so nice to touch, but even better when he flexed them to manhandle me into whatever position he wanted me in right then and there. Ohhhhhh, made me gasp and then do exactly what he asked me to do. I was the best good boy for him. Want me to spread my cheeks, yes sir! Want me to touch my toes, yes sir! Want me to put my mouth to work, yes sir, more please sir!

Finally, FINALLY, when he put on a condom and used more lube than necessary and pushed himself into my ass. Slow. Steady. Checking in with me when all I could do was claw at his shoulders and hold on for dear life.

Finally, he bottomed out and rested balls deep.

"Hmmm," I tried to breathe. He had me on my back, knees pressed to my chest and a pillow shoved under my hips. It was… so much. So much of him everywhere and all at once.

Hot Barista shifted his weight, moved a little. "What's your colour, baby?"

"Green!" I hissed out. "Please move!"

He did. Little rocks, gentle, getting me used to this new feeling. Pressing here and there and everywhere until he found my prostate and my spine lit up suddenly and I moaned.

He stayed right on it. Each rut of his hips into me pressed harder and harder to it.

The bed squeaked.

I was babbling. Begging. Drool spilling from my mouth. "Please… oh God! Fuck me… ugh!"

He dipped in low and kissed me. "Wrong name," he told me.

"What?" I tried to think, but could only scrunch my face as he fucked me more. "Ahh!" Shit, too good!

Panting into my mouth as I moaned, he told me. "If you're calling for God, I'm not fucking you hard enough." And with that, he went to pound town. My poor abused asshole, it can take it! "I want to hear you scream my name," he said.

"Orange!" I forced the word out.

His hips froze and he looked down at me. "What's wrong?"

The switch from being fucked to suddenly being not… whoa, head spin. I blinked at him and breathed for a second there. Felt him start to pull away and quickly grabbed him. "No, don't pull out."

"Baby, what's wrong? Talk to me," he insisted.

"I, um… don'tknowyourname," I said all together.

"What?"

I swallowed hard. How the hell had we gotten to this point? Argh! "I don't know… your name." I admitted.

He stared at me like I was explaining that aliens did exist and I'd let them probe me at some great big probing orgy. Which isn't great. "What do you mean, you don't know my name? We're literally having sex right now."

I spluttered. "I know we are. You're balls deep in my ass. I am well aware of what it is we're doing."

"And you just let someone you don't even know the name of fuck you like this?"

I narrowed my eyes at him, about ready to be pissed off. "What are you implying?"

"That this is ridiculous."

"It's never happened before," I protested.

He leant back from me, sitting on his heels, and still very much inside of me so the shifting felt… good. Must've been unconscious, because he shifted again and rutted his hips. Then shook his head and pulled out.

I moaned at the empty feeling he'd left behind. My knees came together and I whined.

He rubbed soothing circles to my thighs and hips. "What do you call me then?"

"Hot Barista," I admitted with a little laugh.

He chuffed. "Really?"

I nodded.

Then he groaned. As if it was the worst possible name I could've given him after all.

"You never told me your name."

"Rou."

"What?"

"Rou."

I blinked at him. "Yeah? What are you saying?" Why was he just repeating my name?

"My name is Rou."

Blink. Again. Brain not fully working, apparently. I pointed a finger to my chest. "No, my name is Roo."

"What?"

"Roo. Short for Ruben," I introduced myself.

He frowned then snorted a laugh. Pointed at his own chest. "Rou. Not short for anything. It's Japanese."

"Oh… No way," then I dissolved into a giggling fit.

We laughed. He collapsed to the mattress beside me and I crawled into his arms to bury my face into the crook of his neck. "This is so embarrassing!"

"You're embarrassing," he huffed into my ear.

I pulled back. "What have you been calling me all of this time?" Curiosity hitting straight away.

He grimaced.

I poked and prodded his Godly pecs and harassed him until he admitted.

"Cutie," he grumbled.

"Cutie?" I pushed up on his chest looked down at him in judgement. "You think I'm cute."

Again, he groaned and grumbled. But he couldn't deny it.

I teased him non-stop until he shut me up with kissing me. And it went from there. We rolled around, fumbled, added more lube to the mess we'd created before. I whispered to him. "Get inside. Get inside!"

And he slid in hard and deep and soon found his place again on my prostate and a rhythm that left me breathless and gasping into his ear.

"Touch yourself," he ordered me.

I did. Moved my fist to match his pace. Came fast. Spurting all over my chest.

He followed, pushed in deep and gave a punted groan. Then collapsed right on top of me. Smearing the mess further across my chest and splattering it onto his own.

I grimaced.

But held him in my arms as we tried to breathe again like normal people. Inhale and exhale. Normal. Not raggedy and short. Not easy for me when he was so heavy and resting on my prone body. But whatever, it was nice. Sensory wise. To have him on top of me.

I ran my hand up and down his spine. Played with the ends of his hair.

Snorted a half laugh when a thought passed through my empty head.

"What?" his voice was muffled into the pillow beside my head.

"Rou," I tried out the name.

"Hmm?"

"If I call you by my name, will you call me by yours?" I snickered. What kind of idiocy was this turning into? Now we were like the iconic gays?

Rou sighed and pushed up enough to look me in the eye. "No."

I shrugged. "It's going to happen anyway."

"This is stupid," he looked down at the mess. Grimaced. Disengaged from me and walked butt naked from my room. Must've found the bathroom as I heard the tap turn on. He returned with a damp wash cloth.

Loved the view of him naked.

Really loved the view.

He wiped my chest down and then started on some of the mess between my legs.

I winced at how sensitive and sore it all was. "I can do it," and took the cloth from him. "Thanks."

He grunted and collapsed to lay beside me.

I needed a shower. But I also needed cuddles. Tossing the wash cloth to the side, I looked at him with a pout. "Snuggle?"

He nodded and opened his arm up.

I flopped into his hold and just… *hmmm*. Nuzzled his collarbone. Felt good. Satisfied and safe. His arm seat belted me into his side.

"We," his voice rumbled under my ear in his chest. "Suck at communication."

I hummed in agreement. "That we do."

Silence.

Now what? What do we do now?

"How do you spell Rou?" I asked.

"It uses the kanji for wolf," he explained.

"And in English?" Did he mean I had to learn to write his name in Japanese to even be able to spell it?

"R-O-U."

"And it means wolf?"

"The kanji used for it is wolf. If mum had used a different kanji it could mean other things," he said.

"Rou," I practiced. It was weird. I thought my nickname was something strange and I wouldn't come across someone else with a similar name.

"Ruben," he commented. "Is it R-u for Roo?"

I shook my head. "R double o."

"Like kangaroo?"

I groaned and buried my head into his pecs to console myself. "Noooo. There's an asshole at work who uses that logic to call me Skippy."

"Is this the same one we need to poison?"

I nodded.

"Roo," he called my name.

I looked up.

Rou dropped an affectionate kiss to my mouth. Soft. Loving. "Am I staying the night?"

"Hmm, please."

He chuckled and shoved me out of his arms. Cruel. Unfair.

I gaped at him. "What are you doing?!"

"Getting ready for bed," he stretched and scratched his stomach. "Why do you look so distressed?"

"Didn't we just establish that our communication is shit? You shoved me away."

Rou blinked at me. Stared. Blank.

I huffed a sigh and rolled to the other side of the bed so we could pull the sheets down and get organised. Winced as I stood upright. "I'm going for a shower."

As I moved to pass him, Rou grabbed my arm and held me in place. "I know I need to work on communicating as well, but I want to be with you," he told me.

I softened at that. Smiled and stepped into his space and wrapped my arms around him. "It's probably going to take me a while to, um, be able to just say things. It really sucked when you turned me down that last time and I thought it was because I was someone you could fool around with but didn't want to… you know."

His arms tightened around me.

"And I don't know. I'm not brave."

"Hmm?"

I puffed out my cheeks as I tried to find the right words. What were they? "I guess, flirting was something that was easy to do. But I've been wanting to ask you out for a long time. Just didn't have the balls to do it."

"Be my boyfriend," Rou demanded.

My head jerked up at that statement.

He waited.

"Okay," I whispered. "I'd love that. A lot."

He grinned. "Good. Now, can we shower together?"

"Oh? Do you not shower with people who are not your boyfriend?" I teased as I stepped out of his arms and started towards the bathroom. His hand in mine.

"Of course not. I'm a traditional guy."

"What does that even mean?" I laughed, it echoed off the tiles as we entered.

Half an hour later and an empty hot water system, I still had no answer. Instead, I had a hot man sleeping in my bed, naked. Myself, also naked, in his arms and not sleeping.

It was 3am.

My ass had been pounded on this mattress not that long ago. My dick had been jerked off in the shower by the same man. How was I still awake? Shouldn't the hormones or something have plunged me into sleepy oblivion?

No, instead I had the anxiety. Yes, nice to have clarified and made it official that we were boyfriends and that we were a thing. A relationship.

Not a situationship. The real deal.

That was nice and eased some of the stress. Knowing that helped. But… there was a myriad of other things that were… um, not so easily taken care of. The name thing for one. A funny story we'd probably laugh over in years to come even if we broke up. It would still be a nice story to throw out at a party. Like beat that.

But it highlighted some shit. We talked. But didn't really talk talk. And I was honest with not being brave. Being scared to open my mouth and ask him for his number or to ask him out. Hell, even tonight it was him asking to be boyfriends.

I still hadn't said a thing. I just responded.

What is wrong with me? And is it something I can fix? Probably not in a night. Definitely not. But that also meant I wasn't going to be able to settle and sleep.

I sighed and slipped out of Rou's arms and grabbed some pants and a shirt and went out to the lounge. Closed the door so I didn't disturb him.

Ten minutes later and doom scrolling on my phone, Rou stumbled out. Still naked. Still appreciating the view of that.

He frowned at me. "Want me to go?"

I shook my head. "No. Stay. Sleep."

He grunted and came to drop onto the lounge with me. "Why aren't you asleep?"

I shrugged. "Mind won't shut up."

"Anxiety?"

"Something like that."

We sat in silence. I started to wonder if maybe he'd fallen asleep. Was thinking of grabbing him a blanket so he wouldn't catch a cold while sleeping, since there was no way in Hades I was going to be able to princess carry him back to bed. He could do that to me, but not the other way around. I am delicate.

"Talk," he prompted.

I startled. "Thought you'd fallen asleep."

"Talk, Roo. Just say whatever it is you're thinking or feeling."

And in the dark, with him reclining against the back of my lounge and out of my line of sight, I did that. I let it all spill out and didn't feel any better for doing so.

7. I Don't Like Coffee

"The usual?" Rou asked.

I chewed my bottom lip as I stepped up to the counter and put the travel mug down. "No," I answered. "I want to try something else."

Rou's brows shot straight to his hairline. "That's a first. What will it be?"

"Um," now, my eyes darted to the board behind him listing all of the hot beverages they made. This is where the problem had begun. When I'd come in to try the new little café out on the way to work, discovered the barista had been hot, and I panicked and didn't have time nor brain cells to study the board and just blurted something out.

"Would you like a moment?" Rou fucking teased. Asshole.

I glared at him. "Leave me alone," I whined.

"No. Now hurry up, you have work," he chided.

At that I groaned. "I don't wanna go to work," my bottom lip pouted. "Work sucks."

"Quit."

"Ah, yes. Your wise wisdom," I rolled my eyes.

He snorted. "Are you that much of a baby? It's a job, if you don't enjoy it, find something else… unless you're in extreme debt and have to work?"

"Are we talking about our financial situations here and now?" I queried him.

"We've messed up worse things, Roo." The way he said my name was the perfect little reminder that until a few days ago, he hadn't known it.

"No, Rou," I made sure to use his name. "I do not have an outstanding debt that threatens to swallow me whole. Only some HECs debt that the government takes from my salary automatically." I think. I should probably check on that. "I just need to work to be able to live."

At this he smirked. "Then any job that pays is good enough. Find something that you enjoy doing."

"I enjoy you," I fired back. Because I was sick of real talk. I wanted flirting.

"Are you planning on becoming a mattress actress then?"

"A what?" I started to laugh at the ridiculous job title he'd just used. "What did you call it?"

"Mattress actress," he repeated. Calm. Unaffected. Except his eyes flicked up and down my body and he smiled. "You'd be a good one."

"Is my boyfriend encouraging me to make adult films?!"

"Only if you're making them with me."

"Possessive?"

"Very. Now pick a drink!"

I groaned at the order and looked back at the board. "I would like to try…" drew out my words to buy more time. "The hot chocolate."

"Basic."

"Don't be mean to a paying customer who is also your boyfriend," I chided.

He rang me up, took the travel mug and started to work away. "Whip cream?"

"Yes please."

"Marshmallows?"

"Of course!"

He shook his head. "Why am I not surprised? Of course you have a sweet tooth."

I didn't dignify that with a response.

Coming back with my order completed and a random paper packet, Rou placed them on the counter for me. "Didn't feel like coffee?" he asked.

I balked at that question. Oh shit. How do I respond to that and not sound… like an idiot? "Um…" I swallowed hard. "I don't actually like coffee…" I let my words trail off with an awkward laugh.

"Then why has it been your order for months?"

"Because…" *Oh fuck.*

He tossed his head back and laughed at my expense. "You fool," he reached over and gripped the back of my neck and pulled. Planted a big kiss to my mouth. Released me.

I hummed and picked up the travel mug and surprise packet. "I mean, if I wasn't such a fool we wouldn't be together," I fired back at him before escaping the shop.

It was real. This was real. And I was absolutely giddy from it all. Rou was my boyfriend. We'd been able to interact and be all flirty and sweet together after a weekend of fucking like rabbits. I was definitely walking funny today. But… Rou and I were together.

I knew his name.

Hot Barista was upgraded to Rou and though it still was… awkward to use a name so similar to my own, it was so intimate and nice to say his name. Use it to get his attention. Or to chastise him for being mean to me. Or even in bed. That was the most awkward one.

It did feel like I was calling my own name. Maybe I should get people to use Ruben more so Rou was even more special to me to say.

Ugh, sap.

"Morning," I waved at Ronda behind her desk. As always. Paused to have a little chat before taking the elevator up and into hell.

Ash came in minutes after me. "How was your weekend?" they prompted.

I bit my lip. But that was all they needed to figure out that it had been a very good weekend.

Ash squealed and clapped their hands. "Very nice. The barista, right?"

"Oh yeah. He's my boyfriend now," I said with full pride.

"You move fast," they teased. "Once you pull your head out of your ass."

"Had to get it out of there so he could fuck me," I threw back. Sending them into a laughing tizzy.

We sat at our desks, turned on the computers and chatted over the divide as we waited for everything to boot up and be ready to torture us once more.

"What's his name?" Ash asked.

"Rou."

Then they popped up over the divide and stared at me. "Spell it."

"R-o-u."

We both laughed. And it was going to be a normal occurrence now. Every time I introduced him to friends and family, it would be that moment of realising that we had very similar names. Hopefully, it didn't get to be so annoying.

"How old?"

"31."

"He's younger than you?"

"Barely. By a year."

They rapid fired general questions. And they were answers I'd only just learned that weekend because we'd sat down and talked about it and shared basics in what felt like stilted conversation, a job interview for the role of boyfriend.

"Hmmm," Ash disappeared back down on their side of the divide and I heard them start to type away. "Congratulations on the new relationship. I wish you both well."

"Why are you sounding so formal," I complained and opened my emails.

"What? Prefer a fist bump? A 'good job, bro'?"

"Skippy did a good job?"

Ugh.

Good mood vapourised. Destroyed. Like it never existed to begin with. I didn't spin around or acknowledge him, even though I knew Johno was there for me. He never came to harass Ash. Never. And the others he dumped work onto had it done via email and never face to face.

What a ridiculous thing.

The silence stretched.

Ash hadn't responded. And neither did I. What was the point when he was just going to be telling me of all the extra work he was going to be adding to my plate all while calling me a stupid name.

"Hey," he snapped his fingers right by my ear.

I flinched.

"I'm speaking to you," he snapped at me loudly. Catching the attention of everyone nearby.

I spun in my chair to glare up at him. "What is it?"

"Ohhh, someone's in a foul mood this morning," he sneered.

Lord, I hated him. I hated how he got to get away with being such an asshole at work, and yet he could nitpick my every fucking breath, make out like I was the most unreasonable bitch from just a sigh. "What is it?" I repeated.

"I sent you work."

"And?"

"And, have you read the emails?"

"I was doing so when you interrupted."

"No, you were flapping your lips and gossiping about your weekend while on company time," he chastised me.

"I was sharing a conversation with my workmate while waiting for my computer to boot up. Do you want me to wait in silence?" Why are we fighting about something so fucking benign? Casual chatter while the tech gets ready. Everyone does it. It's not stealing on company time.

"I expect you to respond when a manger speaks to you."

Okay, so it's not the chitchat. It's me ignoring him. "How do I know you're talking to me when you didn't say my name?" Two can play this bitchy game. I can be petty. I can soooooo be petty.

"Who else do I call Skippy? Huh? I'm sick of you're utter disregard and acting like you're so perfect."

"Then use my name. If not Roo, then use Ruben. I have a name. I have a preferred nickname. Neither of them are that stupid thing you keep trying to degrade me with," I snapped back.

"It's a name, *Roo*. Get over it." He scoffed. Proved that he also could use my name. "Happy now? Open the damn email."

He hovered over my shoulder as I did so, as I started to read, he breathed down my neck and talked about what he was expecting from me for this part of the job.

It was creepy as fuck! And overbearing.

"Do you understand, Skippy?"

"Crystal." I forced out.

"Good," his smirk could be heard in his tone as he walked away to harass someone else.

I stayed still. My mind was made up. A snap decision is normally made without previous consideration. I've considered this for a long time, but usually with someone else's input. Ash and their bitching. Rou and his simple, one worded advice.

But now… I opened up a new email and started to type.

I regret to inform you that I will be leaving the company.

Added on the exact date I will be terminating my employment with them and then blah blah bullshit about being sad to go and how grateful I was for the job they'd provided. Addressed it to HR and paused to proofread it. Paused to consider.

This wasn't a normal response.

Johno is annoying. Obnoxious. He toed the line with what is acceptable workplace behaviour. The same way my responses back have always toed the line and used what was preached to us as rules to cover my ass. Or used the cover of my manager, Emily, to hide behind.

But every time he'd said something or pushed work onto me. Every time a manager ignored it. Every time the company used rules to punish us, but wanted us to bend them or disregard them completely when it suited the managers. All of those times were small. Little blips, little moments. But they all added up and…

I hit send.

Picked up the phone and called for Emily's office.

"Yes?"

"I don't feel well," I told her. "I need to go home."

"Okay."

I packed up. Everything. Even the little photo strip from my birthday of Ash and I and the rest of our friends in a photo booth acting like idiots that was tacked to my wall. Everything that was mine was coming with me. Turned off my computer.

"What are you doing?" Ash asked. Looking up from their work.

I picked up my travel mug and pastry from Rou. "Going home. I don't feel well. Text me when you're on lunch," I asked them.

They nodded and waved me off.

I walked out of the building and planned to never return.

*

Rou frowned at me as I came into the café. "What are you doing here? You're meant to be at work."

"I quit." Simple. To the point.

"Congrats. Take a seat," he jerked his chin to the table nearest the counter.

I dropped into it and exhaled. Heavy. What had I done? I'd actually done it. I'd quit that job. And not just that, gone home 'sick' instead of dealing with the fallout of that bullshit. If there was going to be any fallout. HR probably wasn't going to give two shits about an office clerk leaving.

Johno couldn't do anything to me for not getting his shitty work done. I wasn't going in the next day. Or the day after that. Shit when was pay day? Were they going to be able to withhold my last pay cheque? Take out bullshit for leaving before certain things were done?

I grabbed out my phone and looked at the calendar. Tomorrow was pay day. Tomorrow I would get my pay from two weeks. Meaning the only thing they could keep hold of was the pay from today. To which, was a sick day any way.

Oh fuck, I need to start looking for a job.

What am I going to do?

"Roo," Rou dropped his hand to my shoulder and grounded me with his touch.

I jolted and looked up at him. "I quit," I repeated again.

He nodded. Dropped down to squat by my chair and look up at me. Took my hand into his. "How are you feeling?"

"Terrified."

"Did something happen at work this morning?"

I explained. And as always, it made it sound like I was blowing it out of proportion. That something so small and irritating was nothing to other people. Maybe I was a snowflake and couldn't be pleased.

Rou's face scrunched up into a frown. "That asshole did what?"

"He hovered over me. Fought me about not responding to that stupid nickname he'd given me. Gave me more work even though I'm not part of his team nor that project."

"I'm amazed you lasted so long at that place," he commented.

A customer came in and he went back to the counter. Leaving me with my thoughts and now the new idea that he'd given me. Maybe Rou was right and it was amazing

I'd lasted that long with all of that bullshit that was happening so consistently. Maybe I wasn't being precious.

Maybe I was justified in leaving.

More customers came in. I stayed in my seat and watched my boyfriend work. He chatted easily with them at the counter. Took their orders to them if they were taking a seat and staying a while.

And every time he moved to pass me, he touched my shoulder.

I drank the hot chocolate from my travel mug, pulled out the little treat he'd given me and snacked on that. Waited for him. Or for my panic to subside enough for me to think for a single moment.

Holy shit, I'd done that.

"Abby, I'm going on break," Rou called to the kitchen and grabbed something to eat before coming to my table and collapsing into the chair opposite me with a sigh. "You okay, baby?" he took my hand and rubbed his thumb over my knuckles.

"I'm unemployed."

He nodded.

"I'm unemployed and don't know what the hell to do. What do I do now? Do I start looking for a job? What am I going to do if I don't find one this month? Or next month?"

"How picky are you about work?" he started to eat.

"What do you mean?"

"Are you willing to take a shitty job in between? Cleaning or working retail or something else?"

I paused and thought about it. "I've never done cleaning before."

"It's an easy enough gig to get. Most people hate to do it so they're always screaming for workers."

I sighed. Sat in silence. Thought. Then started to laugh. "I quit," I said, but this time with that light and airy laugh. "I actually quit that job."

"You did," Rou wiped his mouth with a napkin. "Are you feeling better about it?"

I nodded. "I hated that place and all of the bullshit they did. Always talked about quitting with Ash. But we never did it. Oh fuck, I quit without Ash. They're going to kill me when I tell them," I buried my face into my hands and groaned.

Rou waited for me. He didn't give any input.

"Is it weird that I'm more afraid of what I'm going to do next instead of being happy about leaving a job?" I asked him. Wanting him to give me his input.

He shrugged. "When was the last time you were without a job?"

I thought back. "Some time in uni, I think."

"No wonder you're freaking out," he reached over and with the meat of his palm pressed against my forehead to emphasise. "You've never done this before."

I grabbed his wrist and pulled his hand away from my face and instead held it on the table, twisting our fingers together. "I don't know why but this feels… like it's getting better the more that I sit with it. I quit. I did. I made a choice and went through with it and I'm not going back.

I'm going to call in sick every day until my job is terminated. Ugh, why do I have to give two weeks' notice for such a shitty job? Emily is going to call me and ask me if I'm going to be coming in at all. Do I need to get a doctor's note to explain my absences? Oh fuck me, I should've put in for annual leave or something so I really can just not go back all of this time."

I took a breath. "I think I made a huge mess out of it all."

Rou nodded at that. "Sounds like it."

"Why do you sound so unconcerned?"

He took a sip from his drink and shrugged.

"Is this meant to be like my problem and has nothing to do with you?" I bitched.

"No. It's something affecting you so it concerns me. Just, it's your choice. I'm here for support, baby. Nothing else, unless you want to do that porno." He smirked at me.

I kicked him under the table. "We are not doing a porno." Maybe… it has merit. Work from home. A fun thing to do. I could find a way to make sure I am anonymous. I've seen creators do that before. Some of my favourite videos have no faces in them. "We are not doing porn," I said. More to myself.

Rou huffed a sigh. "I finish at three. Are you planning on sitting and having your mental breakdown here and wait for me? Or are you going home to worry?"

"I'm not worrying." I was. I was worried about how I had just given two weeks' notice instead of telling them to jam it… I pulled out my phone and fired off an email to Emily and HR.

"Hmm?"

"I'm putting in for annual leave for these two weeks as an emergency thing. Maybe it'll work."

Rou waited. "Even if it doesn't, it'll be fine. You'll find a job that isn't going to care about how you left. Or you go back for the next two weeks and finish up. It's all going to be fine." He started to get up and I realised that his break was over and he was going back to work. He dropped a kiss to the top of my head.

Softie.

"I am proud of you," he told me.

And I was happy to admit, that I too was proud of myself.

Emily emailed back fast. My leave was approved. And she commented on my quitting as unfortunate but wished me well with my future endeavours.

Wow.

That just cleared half of my worries. I quit. I left something that wasn't serving me, wasn't making me happy, and now I could very well go and find something that did make me happy to show up and do every day.

And like Rou said, I could have a job in between. I don't have to have the answer right now. I can just be happy to be free and with options and… yeah.

I sighed. Content. *I think I will wait for Rou to finish his shift and then go and do something with him. Be it*

going back to his place to hang out or even going grocery shopping. I'm happy to play it by ear.

8. I Like You

Six months later...

"Happy birthday, Rou," I snuggled into his arms and whispered to him.

Sleepily, he hummed.

The morning was still dark out. It made me want to stay in bed all day and not get out of it for any reason whatsoever. Who needed to go and get to work on time? Not me. I was self-employed. A self-made man, if you will.

I chose my work hours and they did not include working at all this early in the morning. A little bit of work later, but that will be at a more reasonable time.

So I kissed Rou. Noticed that he didn't respond and was probably deep asleep once more. Hmm. I chewed my bottom lip. If he was asleep then this would be a practice run. "I love you, Rou," I whispered. Placed another kiss to his cheek and wanted to bury my face in between his godly pecs and squeal like a fucking fan girl. Jesus.

But the arms tightened around me and Rou kissed me properly on the mouth. "Love you, Ruben," he murmured.

I gaped at him. Awake. Very awake and alert and now slapping the man I adore and love with a pillow because... "I thought you were asleep!"

He grunted and took the hits twice before snatching the pillow away, tossing it from the bed, and restraining me completely. Wrapping his body around mine like a fucking python and squeezing tight. "Stop it. Go to sleep. I love you." He spat out.

I huffed and wanted to protest more. Wanted to bitch about how he was being such a mean man, pretending to sleep while I confessed my love to him. Except… he was really nice to sleep with. Comfortable. Warm. Like, his muscles were strong and he could do a lot with them but they were also not that hard defined rigid sort that look pretty but are not so nice to cuddle.

He was a cuddly buddy.

So I slept again. Dozed off in his arms for a while until he was waking me with sweet kisses and words. "Baby," he said. "Get up."

"Hmmmm?" I groaned and burrowed back into the blankets.

"Don't you want to get up and give me my present?" He tugged on the blanket. A warning tug. The cruel man would be ripping it from the bed soon and leave me helpless and exposed to the harsh weather.

"Who says I got you anything," I complained.

"Baby," he warned one last time.

The blankets went flying from the bed and I yelped at the sudden drop in temperature around my body. "Rou! Asshole! Don't be so mean."

"Get up," he ordered. Completely dressed and heading out of the bedroom.

I glared at him, then looked at my phone for the time. "Shit, why is it so late?" I vaulted from the bed and into clothes.

"We slept in," he announced from the kitchen.

I flounced in and dropped to the kitchen bench. "How long have you been awake?"

"An hour or so," he placed a plate of food in front of me. "Eat. You're going to need your energy."

"Do you have plans for me tonight?" I asked. All innocence gone. Pure flirty whore.

He scoffed.

I stuffed my face with the steaming pile of hot breakfast. Eggs and sausages and toast. All of the good stuff. "Have you eaten?" I noted as he sat beside me and only drank his coffee.

"Hmm."

"Why didn't you wake me earlier?"

"You needed the sleep."

"But it's your birthday and I should be pampering you with breakfast in bed," I swiped my mouth with the back of my hand and pouted. "Happy birthday."

"You already said that," dropped a kiss to my nose. Making me scrunch it up in response.

"Wasn't sure you heard that one. You were half asleep."

"I heard. And I heard you say the other thing."

My face felt hot and I'm sure I was blushing. Shit. "You said it back," I mumbled.

He nodded his head and sipped. "I love you."

My head jerked up and stared at him. My heart squeezing tight with the fact this man was my boyfriend. He loved me. "I love you," I replied.

And I don't know when but I want to make it perma-
nent and official. If we make it past our first year, I want
to put a ring on it. A year of courtship is a decent amount
of time. You can learn a lot about a person in one year and
whether or not you want to spend the rest of your life with
them as a life partner or if you'd prefer to part ways.

"So, where's my present?" he asked. Again. And obnoxious about it.

"God, you're like a kid demanding their present instead
of being happy they've been allowed to make it to another
year," I grumbled.

"What are you suggesting?"

"Your entitlement is showing." I moved around the
kitchen and plopped the plate into the sink for later. "And
I don't think you deserve your gift."

Rou quirked his brow. "How would you like me to act
for it, hmm?"

"Patience is a virtue," I teased.

"Not right now it isn't," he quoted and got up to chase
me and crowd me against the bench top. Looming. Arms
boxing me in.

And ohh, that thrill zinging up my spine. Please, sir!
Dominate!

"What have you got for me, baby?"

I wet my lips and grabbed his hips to encourage him to
press against me, lean his weight onto me and hmmm, just
like that. Could feel his dick filling out as we touched and
played this ridiculous game of flirting. "It's on my computer," I told him.

Right before he dipped down and planted a kiss to my lips. Stole any and all other words from me. Fuck me! Yes, please! I looped my arms around his neck.

At the solid feel of his hands on my waist, I jumped up, he took most of my weight easily, and I wrapped my legs about his midsection. Clung to him like a horny koala.

He started walking.

"Where are we going?" I gasped when I realised it wasn't back to the bedroom.

"Your computer," he nipped my jaw. "I want to see my present."

"I hope you like it," I winced a little. If he didn't or thought it was tacky for a gift… I don't know what else to do. It had been such a great idea and I wanted to give him something special. But still, who gave a sex tape for a birthday gift?!

This fool.

Rou sat on the office chair and kept me on his lap as he booted up my computer and used the password to log in. "Where is it?" One hand stayed on my lower back. Stroking. Fingers dipping low and into the waistband of my pants.

I wiggled around and took the mouse. It was an awkward angle to see the screen and open the file. But I managed. The video started to play.

And like with all other videos of me in them, I hated hearing my voice. Not that hiding my head into the crook of his neck was going to stop me from hearing, but it was going to be one of the few little things I could do to comfort myself without leaving the room and letting him watch it alone.

It was solo play.

My face was off camera and the few times it dipped into frame I blurred my features to be unrecognisable.

I could hear my breath catching in the video. My moans and whines getting more frantic as I played with myself.

But it was the hard cock I was sitting on that I cared about the most. The feel of Rou's hand gripping my ass and encouraging my hips to move, to slide up and down against him, to hump his dick with mine.

I gasped in real life along with the video of me. "Rou?"

"Hmm, oh baby. Play for me now."

And I did. I shoved my pants down and under my ass, tugged him out of his pants. Licked my palm. Lined our cocks together and started to stroke. Not in time with the video that had finished and with a sharp click from Rou, started again. No, I moved lazily. Wanting him to lose control and to demand it fast. Or to just lift me up and spear my ass with his dick.

He did none of those things. He took what I was giving.

I whined.

"Hmm?" he prompted.

"Don't you want me to go faster?" Or to possibly fuck me?

He chuckled and kissed my neck. "This is my birthday present. You're the one giving it to me."

Ohhhh, asshole. But my hand sped up. My free hand gripped his hair and brought his mouth back to mine. Soon I was coming. And then he followed. Our kissing became lazy.

On the screen, I came, again.

I rested my forehead against his, tried to catch my breath. "Are you happy with your gift?"

"Very," he hugged me tight. Not caring about the mess between us. "I like it."

"You don't think it's weird to give a sex tape for a birthday?" Still, a little unsure.

"All I'll say is, I would like to make a sex tape for my next birthday," and he chuckled as I hid in the crook of his neck. "Baby is so shy. Even though you're not shy in front of the camera."

"Ugh! Leave me alone."

"Nope. Have you uploaded this one online?" he asked. His hand rubbed up and down my back.

I shook my head. "Wanted it to be for you to see first. I'll post it later."

"Good. They're going to eat this shit up. You're so hot, baby," he praised me.

And I pulled back to look at him and grinned. "I don't know if I can be compared to the Hot Barista. He's pretty fucking hot," was all I got out before shrieking as he tickled me.

Hello,

Thank you for reading. I hope you enjoyed I Don't Like Coffee, I Like You.
I would much appreciate it if you did leave an honest review wherever you like to leave reviews.
If you would like to read more head to
aprilklasenbooks.weebly.com
Happy reading,
April

Independently published author. Artist. BL and fanfic whore. April Klasen lives in regional NSW Australia. Find her @defiantdame on most social media sites or sign up for the book newsletter at aprilklasenbooks.weebly.com

More books are coming.

Also by April Klasen

Romance:
I Don't Like Coffee, I Like You
Fitz: A Queer Pride & Prejudice Retelling
Pure Pop Asia
I Heart Pop Asia
Summertime Madness
Hook-up or Date

Fantasy:
A Witch's Wand
The Annual
Beta
Blair: Salem's Daughter
Blair: The Sleeping Daughter
Blair: The Same Daughter

Coffee
apaccino
Latte
Mocha
Espresso
Pot of tea
Bl
Call me xx
April Klassen

OSED
PULL

9 781923 217966